D0835531

12429789

Wild Justice

When five men, led by notorious killer Ernest Jones, flee from a posse, they cause untold havoc and destruction. After killing a farmer and ravishing his daughter Gwendolyn, they flee. The ordeal has left Gwendolyn with a thirst for vengeance and, concealing her gender, she rides out in hot pursuit. Finding a job with Sheriff Humphrey Quigley, Gwendolyn is persuaded to infiltrate the Jones gang in order to deliver them to the sheriff and to the gallows.

But violence and death dog every step as Gwendolyn fights to survive among the brutal outlaws, whose motto is shoot first and fast. Can she keep her identity secret long enough to bring these thugs to justice?

Wild Justice

P. McCormac

A Black Horse Western

ROBERT HALE · LONDON

© P. McCormac 2012
First published in Great Britain 2012

ISBN 978-0-7090-9817-1

Robert Hale Limited
Clerkenwell House
Clerkenwell Green
London EC1R 0HT

www.halebooks.com

The right of P. McCormac to be identified as
author of this work has been asserted by him
in accordance with the Copyright, Designs and
Patents Act 1988
Typeset by
Derek Doyle & Associates, Shaw Heath
Printed and bound in Great Britain by
CPI Antony Rowe, Chippenham and Eastbourne

1

'Pa, someone's coming.'

Gwendolyn pushed back her hair and shaded her eyes as she peered out past the corral. She observed the dust cloud in the distance as riders spurred towards their homestead. From the amount of dirt kicked up she surmised there were at least half a dozen of them.

Percival Caruthers heard his daughter calling and paused in his work. He wiped the sweat from his brow. It was a hot day as was every day once summer began. The naked sun burned remorselessly as father and daughter laboured on the smallholding, each at their separate tasks; he trimming the hoofs of his ancient mule, while Gwendolyn washed and chopped vegetables for the evening meal.

Gwendolyn was working by the well. She had propped a board on the sod wall of the well and diced up the turnip and jerky for the pot. She could feel the sweat breaking on her body and damp patches showed on her armpits and on the small of her back. When she was satisfied with the broth she would take the heavy iron pot inside the house and place it on the stove where it would slowly cook. The resulting glutinous mess would be dished up with fresh-baked sour-dough bread.

Percival Caruthers came and stood beside his daughter

and looked out at the dust cloud. He was a lean man, not old but aged by the hard life eking a living from his smallholding. His grey hair was long and hung untidily around his ears and neck.

The Caruthers had so few visitors the activity out on the prairie was a source of curiosity. So they stood together, father and daughter, and watched the dust thrown up by the horsemen approaching their humble dwelling not knowing that this day their lives would be changed forever.

On they came, five men pulling up their tired mounts in a cloud of dust. The men looked weary, worn-out and travel-stained and not showing much friendliness. They sat their horses by the corral and looked over at the pair in the yard. Hard to tell if they were glad to arrive or just too fatigued to summon the energy for a greeting.

'Howdy, fellas,' Percival Caruthers called out. 'You need water; we got a good well. Just help yourselves.'

There was no reply but the riders dismounted and one by one hitched their mounts to the top rail of the corral. As they stepped across to enter the yard and approach the couple waiting to meet them they were slapping at clothing sending small puffs of dust floating into the still, hot air.

Percival Caruthers had a small niggle of unease as the men approached. The strangers had dour unsmiling faces but the most disturbing thing about the gang was the amount of hardware they were toting on their persons. Without exception all had six-guns strapped on their hips and some had bandoleers of ammunition slung across their chests.

Gwendolyn was intrigued at the sight of so many men suddenly appearing out of the blue and descending on their lonely farm. Visitors were rare. The occasional drummer or wagons on the way through to a new life further west was about the extent of new faces seen around the smallholding. So the sudden influx of five strangers was a mild excitement for the young girl.

Gwendolyn had just turned eighteen and still had the body of a youngster not long out of puberty. Hard work and poor fare had kept her body slim and boyish so she had still not developed the breasts and hips of women in a less straitened way of life.

So exacting was the work she had been doing almost from when she could toddle as she helped her mother at the various tasks a frontier woman must accomplish that Gwendolyn's body was as wiry and strong as any boy of similar age. She stood with all the innocence of an adolescent girl and watched with interest as the five rough-looking strangers approached.

'You alone here?'

The man that spoke was the oldest of the group; his skin leathery and wrinkled with a slash for a mouth. The voice was coarse and roughened as of a man who had smoked his way through countless sacks of Bull Durham.

'Why, yeah,' Caruthers answered. 'There's just the two of us. We ain't got much but you're sure welcome to share what we got.'

There was a slight quiver in Caruthers' voice as he began to feel the first twinges of unease. Indeed there was something intimidating about the behaviour of the five men. There was no greeting and other than that question from the older man while his companions maintained a brooding silence staring sullenly at the farmer and his daughter.

'Mike, look inside.'

A heavily built man with a broad face adorned with a partial beard on his chin and upper lip broke from the group and stalked across to the house. As he approached the open front door he pulled a pistol before disappearing inside.

'What's all this about, fella?' As he spoke Caruthers stepped forward a pace so his daughter was behind him as if wanting to place himself between her and these strangers who were making the air cold with unspoken menace in spite of the hot sun. 'We ain't got nothing worth stealing if that's what you're after.'

The old man's eyes slid past the dirt farmer towards the girl standing behind him.

'My men have been riding hard. We ain't stopped riding for three days. I guess we're entitled to a break afore we have to set off again.'

'Mister, you're welcome to water but beyond that there's nothing here for you or your men. As soon as you've watered up I want you to ride on.'

'The place is empty like he says.'

The burly man was standing in the doorway still holding his pistol awaiting further instructions.

'Ernest, that young filly looks ready for breaking.'

'Yeah, I reckon she's got enough sauce in her for all of us.'

'OK, I'll keep watch. But I think we lost that posse long days back. Take her in the house.'

They were talking amongst themselves without regard as to whether the girl or her father might have any objection to their actions; as if the girl was an inanimate object with no say-so in the matter.

'Yippee!'

They surged forward, their erstwhile tiredness forgotten. Like a startled animal or bird frightened at the sudden onrush, Gwendolyn instinctively stepped back, her eyes wide with panic as she saw in the eyes of these rough newcomers an expression that frightened her.

'Damnit to hell. . . .' Percival Caruthers raised his arms and his voice. 'For God's sake, what are you doing?'

A shot rang out and the farmer staggered back clutching his bloodied chest.

'Pa!'

Gwendolyn screamed as she saw her father stagger back and lean drunkenly against the well. She jumped forward to assist him but a pair of brawny arms wrapped around her, halting her forward movement. Rough bristles chaffed her neck as the man's face nuzzled her.

'It's all right, honey; just you come in the house with us.'

Without a backward glance or a twinge of conscience at the devastation they had visited upon the little family these brutal men mounted up and filed out of the yard to continue their journey.

For long moments nothing stirred in that yard or house. The sun beat down on the man sprawled in the dirt, his shirt dark with blood. Inside the house the young woman lay on the floor barely conscious. Then the flickering of awareness began to seep through the dark mists that blotted out the pain and humiliation of her ordeal. Life guttered back into that ravaged body at first in stuttering sparks of pain and undertones of terror.

'Noooo . . .' the sound sighed from her ruined lips, but consciousness like a great beast lurking with opened maw awakened and the world of pain and nightmare cruelly bared itself to that delicate creature so brutally abused.

'Pa . . .' she called feebly as memory returned along with the agony. 'Pa. . . .'

Even as the pain grew along with her awareness she knew her father's need was greater, for she had witnessed the callous action as the leader of the bandits gunned him down.

Gwendolyn struggled to her feet, donned her torn shirt and pulled on her pants to cover her ravaged body. She staggered to the door and lent against the frame peering out into the yard fearing what she would see. A moan of anguish broke from her as she saw the bloodied form of her father stretched upon the dirt.

'Oh, Pa . . .' she whispered hoarsely then stopped.

Percival Caruthers looked like a dead man and watching over him was another presence in the yard. A vile and sinister shape perched atop the well.

2

The head of the vulture turned and beady eyes regarded this new creature smelling of blood that had appeared in the doorway. Even as Gwendolyn watched, a shadow glided across the yard and another bloated shape landed near the body of the farmer.

'Get away,' Gwendolyn called hoarsely.

The huge birds of death gazed back at the girl, sensing her weakness and marking her for their next meal. There was an almost silent movement and a third evil bird flew into the yard. Gwendolyn looked round for a weapon. The only thing she could see was the broom she used for sweeping the floor of their little house.

She picked it up and in her weakened state it felt heavy and unwieldy in her hands. Holding the broom before her she ventured out to do battle with the vile birds.

'Shoo,' she called and waved the broom.

The carrion eaters shifted uneasily. Reluctantly the evil trio retreated before the girl. And then their bravado evaporated as Gwendolyn found her voice.

'Go away! There is nothing for you here!'

And they went, flapping awkwardly with their huge wings,

glaring balefully till they were airborne. Discarding her impromptu weapon Gwendolyn dropped to her knees beside the outstretched the body of her father.

'Pa, Pa, I'm so sorry.'

Ignoring the blood on his shirt she put her arms around him and wept bitterly. Great sobs racked her body and she sobbed for herself, and for the terrible thing that had happened to her father. And in the midst of her grief there was a faint whisper from the man. Gwendolyn grew still.

'Pa.' She put her hands on his cheeks and gazed Ernestly into his face. 'Pa.' There came again a faint sigh and Gwendolyn placed her ear against his bloody chest and discerned the faint heartbeat. 'Oh thank God, you're alive.'

Gwendolyn knew the first thing she had to do was to get her father into the shade of the well. The girl was of slender build but this belied a strength she had built up from the hard work she had to do on the smallholding. Chopping wood, carrying heavy pails of water, hoeing vegetables and ploughing the fields had endowed her with strength far beyond her town-bred sisters. Even so, weakened by the cruel ordeal at the hands of the outlaws she found it no easy task to drag her father the few yards into shelter.

'Pa, don't die on me. I'm going to make you well again.'

She went back to the cabin and brought blankets and cotton cloths and tried to make her father comfortable. Then she began the harrowing task of unfastening his blood-drenched shirt exposing the wound in his chest. Steeling herself against the sight of the blood she drew a pail of water and began the arduous task of cleansing the wound. But first she carried water inside and set it to heat on the stove.

Tenderly she washed his upper body and while she toiled she talked to her injured parent.

'Pa, I hope I'm not hurting you. I'm being as gentle as I can.'

Gwendolyn worked steadily, trying to ignore her own hurts as she laboured over her father. Gently she swabbed away the bloodstains from around the wound, a small dark and sinister hole in her father's chest.

'Just you hold on there, Pa. You're going to be fine. You know I can't run this farm on my own. We'll have to plough the fields soon for planting the wheat.'

Gwendolyn placed clean pads across the wound and sat back on her heels, regarding her work.

'Pa, I've got to get you turned so as I can see if that bullet has gone through and patch you up some on your back.'

It was harrowing work to get her father on his side. She cut the shirt away to save the distress of trying to remove the garment from the unconscious man. To her consternation she could see no evidence of an exit wound. She sat there staring at the bared skin and then noticed a small protrusion with dark bruising around it. Reaching out she gently probed the lump with her finger. The swelling was hard with no give in it.

'Pa, I think I've found the bullet. It ain't gone through but I think it's there just under the skin. I reckon I'll have to cut it out.'

As Gwendolyn walked across the yard to the house her legs trembled beneath her. She tried to ignore her own injuries. Inside the house she had to resist the temptation to go in the bedroom and crawl under the covers and never have to come out again.

Kettles of water were steaming on the stove and she filled a basin and dropped in a thin sharp knife. For a moment a wave of weakness almost overwhelmed her and she had to rest her hands on the table to stay upright.

'Gwendolyn, Pa needs you,' she whispered. 'He's lying out there with a bullet in him and you got to be strong and dig it out.'

Back outside again Gwendolyn set the steaming basin on the ground and knelt. For a moment as she contemplated what she had to do, she closed her eyes and a wave of faintness swept through her.

'No,' she said fiercely. 'I can do this.'

She raised her eyes to the incandescent sky with that remorseless sun.

'Dear God, if you are up there, help me do this. I can't do it on my own. I need your help.'

3

Darkness had fallen on the little homestead. Faint yellow light seeped out from the humble house made of sods that had been dug from the prairie by Percival Caruthers and his wife, Lorna, who had assisted him at the tough labouring involved in building a home in what was a wilderness. Lorna had been with child when they finished the house. Her daughter was born in that lonely place but Lorna had only five years of motherhood to enjoy before succumbing to illness one severe winter when the cold bit hard and killed humans as well as animals.

Inside the cabin Gwendolyn stood naked beside a tub of water from which rose faint wisps of steam. Ignoring the pain of the wounds inflicted on her delicate skin she scoured her body causing the bites and abrasions to bleed freely, as if by this sacrifice of blood it would make her clean again. If this was her intention it did not succeed for she was filled with loathing and hatred – loathing for herself and

13

hatred for the men who had abused her and shot her father.

Gwendolyn, the innocent youngster who had so patiently worked beside her father was dead. She had been buried by a gang of outlaws who had swept through her peaceful life, shot her father and obliterated her youth and innocence. She felt she was dirtied and would never be clean again as she scoured the old Gwendolyn away and in its place a new version emerged. Where before there had been tenderness now there was emptiness; where before there was trust now there was wariness and underlying was a need for vengeance.

Once she was dressed in clean clothing she took the old rifle from the pegs above the door. She was familiar with the gun for Percival had showed her how to clean and load and fire it. Even so, on the occasions he had taken his daughter with him on his hunting trips she had never been able to bring herself to shoot the animals they stalked. Now she held the rifle and it had become a killing thing in her hands. She was sure in her mind she would be able to kill. Today's events had destroyed all her former inhibitions. Gathering blankets from the bed she walked out to the well where her wounded father was lying.

'Pa, I'm here. I'm going to look after you.'

She settled down near him, resting her back against the well, the rifle propped beside her and the sharp knife she had used earlier to cut the bullet from her father jammed in a crack within easy reach. If marauders were to descend again upon their homestead Gwendolyn Caruthers was not going to be caught unprepared.

Now she was set to spend the night beside her wounded father to protect him from predators. The image of the vultures with their cruel beaks waiting to drop on the helpless man was one she remembered with horror. The terrible experiences of the day pressed upon her and she felt tears well up.

'Pa,' she whimpered, 'why did those men do those things to us? We never harmed no one.'

The night closed down, drawing a star-studded canvas across the sky. Night creatures crept from their burrows. The hunters were out stalking their next meal. Coyotes barked and somewhere out in the distance a wolf howled to be answered from afar.

Gwendolyn listened to these familiar sounds with aching heart and bruised body and with weapons near at hand kept watch. She was determined no man or beast would harm her father while she watched over him. But the terrors of her ordeal and her battered and aching body cried out for sleep – healing sleep that would blot out the nightmare of the waking memories.

Exhaustion of mind and body worked upon her and she dozed while the night closed in around her. It was not to be a peaceful sleep for she tossed and turned, her fevered brain reliving the terrors of her ordeal at the hands of the gang that had burst so violently into their peaceful life.

Far out in the prairie a group of riders saw the faint glow of light in the distance and turned their horses in that direction. Gwendolyn slept on oblivious of the second band of horsemen about to invade their homestead.

4

The saloon was noisy with boisterous revellers. The gaming tables were busy and the bartenders were hard at work serving thirsty customers. Gaudily dressed and overly painted ladies plied their trade, cajoling men to buy drinks as well as coaxing them upstairs to the bedrooms of desire.

'Ben – Ben Truman.'

A young man turned his head from where he was engaged in a game of poker and saw his friend Terry Wilkes pushing through the crowd trying to catch his attention.

'Pardon me, gentlemen.' Ben threw in his hand. 'I fold.'

Ben had been losing steadily and was glad of the excuse to quit the game. He was not aware he was being cheated by two of the players, who worked together and were in the practice of fleecing naive young men with more money than sense.

'Ben, you got to help me,' Terry said excitedly and grabbed Ben by the arm.

'Wow, Terry, you gone and got some gal in trouble and you want me to take the blame?'

'Ben, be serious, I need you to come with me when I go courting Miss Eliza Donohue.'

'Miss Eliza Donohue! You're daft. She'll never look twice at you. Why, half Prestwick County is chasing after Miss Eliza.' Ben looked his friend up and down, suddenly noticing something different about him. 'Hell, you got on new duds?' Ben had only ever seen his pal in his cheap suit but now Terry was attired in a leather vest and a smart shirt with good cord trousers and a silver-studded belt. Ben whistled. 'You embezzled money from the bank, Terry? Don't worry; you can hole up at my place. When the sheriff comes looking we'll fight him off.'

'Goddamnit, Ben, will you be serious for once in your life? My whole future will be in jeopardy if you don't help me.'

Terry grabbed Ben's arm and dragged his pal through the crowded room till he got them both outside. Terry was slim and narrow-faced with long black hair. In contrast, Ben

16

Truman was of sturdy build with hair shorn short that in certain lights was almost golden. The two had been pals since attending the school ruled over by Miss Heffner, a stern spinster who took no nonsense from the boisterous boys under her charge.

'I been saving my wages,' Terry began earnestly, 'till I had enough to pay for these duds. I reckoned Miss Eliza would take notice of me if I showed her I weren't just a rough no-account bum like you, Ben Truman. She's bound to pay me some mind when I turn up dressed like an English lord.'

Ben chuckled. 'An English lord! You look and smell more like an English pimp.'

'Damnit Ben, the store clerk told me this is what the English aristocracy wear. My future happiness and Eliza's depends on me going over to her place tonight and plighting my troth.'

'Plighting your troth.' Ben was trying to suppress his laughter without much success. 'Holy cow, Terry, that sounds serious. What the hell sort of stuff you been reading? And what's all this English stuff anyway. My guess some of that lotion you plastered on your hair has affected your brain. Do you feel a mite dizzy?' Ben took his friend's arm and tried to pull him back into the saloon. 'I reckon a few shots of bourbon will bring you to your senses.'

'Damn you, Ben!' Terry shook off his pal's grip. 'I'm serious. I need you to be there in case I freeze. I love that gal, Ben. I'll do anything to get her to notice me. I'm all ate up inside about her. I know I ain't got much to offer a woman like Miss Eliza but perhaps if I call on her once in a while she will grow to like me. I could take her riding. And we could walk out together.'

Detecting the earnestness of his pal's pleading, Ben, too, became serious.

'Hell, Terry, I can see you got a bee in your bonnet over

17

this. OK, I'll do what I can to help. Let's think out a plan of attack.'

'It ain't no attack, Ben, it's got to be a gentle approach, can't you see that?'

'OK, OK, I'm on it. It'll be like stalking a deer; slow and gentle and cautious.'

'Yeah, something like that. Yeah, I like that gentle and slow bit. How do I go about it?'

'First thing you got to bring her a gift. A bottle of moonshine would do the trick. Get her drunk and she'll do anything for you.'

'Hells bells, Ben, what sort of a fella you think I am? Miss Eliza is respectable. She ain't going to want no moonshine. And I ain't getting her drunk neither. I expected some help from you and all you do is come up with moonshine and getting a girl drunk.'

'All right then, no moonshine. How's about you bring her flowers? Women always like flowers. It's the smell or something that does it.'

'Flowers, where the hell am I going to get flowers at this time of night?'

'The cemetery, there's always flowers out on boot hill. We go grab a bunch of flowers from there and Miss Eliza will be cock-a-hoop when you arrive with a spray of sweet smelling blooms. Good job you came to see me. Wily Ben Truman always has the answer.'

'Ben, we can't go robbing no cemetery. What'll Miss Eliza think when I arrive with a bunch of flowers stolen off someone's grave? "Miss Eliza, I just went to boot hill for these flowers. I wish Ben Truman was up there now with me piling sods on top of him for coming up with such a crazy idea".'

'Damnit, Terry, flowers is flowers no matter where they come from. Don't you think the people that put those

flowers there have to pick them from someone's garden?
More and likely they steal them if they ain't got a garden of
their own. So you'd only be moving them around.'

'Somehow it doesn't seem right stealing from the dead.'

'Remember this, Terry Wilkes,' Ben said in sepulchral
tones, 'dead men tell no tales.'

In spite of his agitated state, Terry couldn't help smiling.

'All right, Ben. I'll do it. I suppose I can't go courting
empty-handed.'

5

Eliza Donohue's father was the mayor of Downsville and
owner of several lucrative businesses connected to the area.
He was the president of the bank where Ben and Terry
worked; Terry as clerk and Ben as security guard. The family
lived in a mansion on the outskirts of Downsville. When the
two pals rode up to the big house everywhere seemed
strangely quiet.

'You think anyone is at home?' Terry asked nervously. He
clutched a cluster of flowers fixed on a frame woven into the
shape of a heart.

'Miss Eliza is going to drop dead at your feet when you
present her with this.'

Terry had been too keyed up to appreciate his friend's
graveyard humour.

'What'll I say?' Terry asked, suddenly nervous as they
hitched their mounts to the rail before the house.

'Miss Eliza, please accept this heart to remind you of my

own heart which you already have in your possession.'

Terry turned to his friend. 'Damn me, Ben, if that don't sound real good.'

'She'll throw her arms around you and clasp you to her bosom so she can feel your heart beating madly for love of her very own self.'

'I can't do it, Ben. Let's go back to town.'

'Terry, don't you chicken out on me now. After all the trouble I went to robbing graves and all.' Ben grabbed his pal by the arm. 'You march right up to that door and knock.'

'I'm scared, Ben. What if she doesn't like the flowers? What if she doesn't like me?'

Terry tried to turn around but Ben had a firm grip on him.

'You're going to knock that door or I'll rope you to this hitching rail and go back to town and leave you to explain to Miss Eliza why you are tied up outside her house. You knock that door now.'

'OK, OK. Just give me a minute or two.'

'Now, Terry Wilkes, now!'

So Terry, the nervous suitor, mounted the porch and timidly knocked on the front door of the Donohue mansion. The place seemed eerily quiet as the two pals stood waiting for a response to their knock.

'There ain't anyone at home,' Terry said, relieved.

'It ain't late enough for them to be in bed,' Ben speculated. 'Maybe they're out back having supper. You stay here in case someone comes to the door while I go around and see if I can rouse anyone.'

Ben stuck his hands in his pockets and sauntered down the side of the house.

'What the hell am I doing out here on this fool errand,' Ben muttered and kicked at a pebble. 'I could be back at the Ace of Spades winning a fortune at poker.' But then he thought of Terry standing nervously at the front door of the Donohue residence with a heart-shaped wreath from the local cemetery and he chuckled. 'Hell, a man has to stand by his buddy. Terry would do the same for me.'

Ben rounded the corner of the house and was looking for signs of life. There were no lights anywhere and Ben stood for a moment at a loss. A large glass-panelled edifice had been erected some distance from the house and Ben stood gazing in admiration at it.

'Donohues sure live high on the hog, as my old pa used to say,' Ben mused.

This got him thinking of the wealth Pierce Donohue had accumulated over the years. Rumours circulated that his success was down to ruthless behaviour that steamrollered over business rivals. Ben had heard tales from old-timers how Donohue had swallowed up business after business when the owners defaulted on loan payments. Seeing as Donohue owned the bank it wasn't too hard to see how this would be accomplished. And yet his pal Terry Wilkes aspired to court the daughter of this wealthy baron.

'I guess love does something to a fella's brain.'

Stars flooded the night sky and bathed the surroundings with a pallid luminescence that seemed almost ghostly. As he stood lost in speculation regarding his friend's predicament Ben thought he detected movement inside the glasshouse. He frowned and squinted in an attempt to see better in the uncertain light and then moved forward, straining his eyes to see what had caught his attention.

The glass reflecting the starlight made it difficult to make out anything within the building. Ben leaned against the glass pane, placed his hand above his eyes and peered inside. At first he could detect nothing as his eyes adjusted to the dim-lit interior. But there was definite movement within, which had caught his attention.

Ben was about to rap on the glass but thought better of it and instead looked for a door into the glass-panelled edifice. He moved around, grasped the door handle rapped his knuckles against the glass and pushed it open. There was a gasp and a hurried movement within. Ben stopped, his jaw agape as he saw the partially clothed man and woman hastily covering up their state of undress.

'Jeez, I'm sorry,' he stuttered. 'I . . . didn't mean to interrupt.' Ben was backing out of the doorway when he suddenly stopped as he realized the identity of the woman. 'Miss Eliza . . . I . . . I. . . .'

'Wait, Ben,' Eliza Donohue called. 'Ben, it's not what you think. In spite of what you see there was nothing improper going on. Can't you see that? I know how it looks but I can explain.'

Eliza advanced towards Ben who was still hovering in the doorway not sure whether to take flight or to stay.

'I . . . never saw nothing, Miss Eliza,' Ben mumbled.

By now Eliza was very close. Ben took no notice of the man moving to the side as if to escape through the door. He could only stare at Eliza and with the thought of Terry at the front door with a bouquet of flowers for her. How was he going to tell his friend of what he had seen? There was a sudden movement beside Ben and before he could react he was grabbed and pulled inside and something smashed into the side of his head. The blow was so forceful Ben could feel his knees buckle.

'You'll not say anything, because you won't be able to,' a voice snarled.

A second blow with the butt of the man's pistol and Ben was slipping into unconsciousness.

'Brendan, why did you do that?' Eliza asked in a scared voice.

'Goddamn it, you know why. If he blabs what he saw we're

in trouble. You know we can't be seen together. Your pa will have me horsewhipped if not hanged. I ain't getting in trouble for the sake of some goddamn peeping-tom. I'll take him outside of town and finish him off.'

'No, oh dear God, no. You can't kill him.'

'We've no other option. It's my life or his.'

6

The nightmare was back. Gwendolyn could see the dark threatening figures gathered around her. Somehow they had returned under cover of darkness and her ordeal would begin all over again. She must have fallen asleep. How could she have let her guard down so badly?

One of the outlaws was crouched down beside her, nudging her foot. She pretended to be still asleep. The gun! It would take too long to grab and line it up on them. The knife was nearby, wedged in a crack in the wall.

'Wha—.'

She moved slowly as if still not quite awake stretching her arms, her hand touching the handle of the knife.

'Are you hurt?'

Gwendolyn slashed out with the knife.

'Jeez!'

The man's hand came up to block the blow and the knife sliced into his sleeve. He fell backwards scrambling to get away from the blade.

'Goddamn, he's cut me!'

'Hold off there, fella. We ain't going to harm you.'

Now that the man had fallen back Gwendolyn lunged for the rifle. A dark form came at her and a hand grabbed the barrel before she could bring it to bear. She dragged at the weapon and the man holding the barrel had a hard time keeping it turned towards the sky.

'Goddamnit, fella, will you stop fighting!'

But she wouldn't cease kicking and trying to wrench back her rifle and blast these devils to kingdom come.

'Someone give me a hand here.'

Two more came forward and pushed her on her back. One knelt on her chest while the man who grasped the rifle prised it from her grip. She sobbed then as she realized the horror was about to begin all over again but still she fought them.

'Will you give over? Don't have me shoot you to quiet you.'

'Shoot me then,' she sobbed. 'Shoot me now and get it over with.'

'Hang on, this ain't no fella. I'm thinking this is a gal.'

'A gal, well dang my hide!'

'Ain't no gal that. She's a devil out of hell. My arm's bleeding where she cut me.'

'OK fellas, I got the gun. Let's all step back and see if she calms down a mite.'

Suddenly she was free. Gwendolyn looked round wildly for a weapon but they had taken the knife as well as the gun. They stood round in a circle watching her. Once more she was helpless before these brutes. She glared up at them like a wild animal at bay.

'Look, miss, whatever you think, we ain't going to harm you. This here is a posse. We been trailing a bunch of outlaws but lost their trail in the dark. When we saw your light we naturally headed here. Look, here's my badge. I'm Marshal Quigley.'

In the dim light she stared at the metal disk the man was indicating on his vest.

'Posse . . . lawmen. . . .' She stared up at them confused.

'There's a fella here looks likc hc's in a bad way.'

Someone was kneeling beside Percival Caruthers.

'What happened here, miss? Did a bunch of hellions come this way?'

'Yes,' she whispered so low the marshal had to bend low to hear her. 'They shot my pa.'

The lawman straightened.

'Some of you men carry that wounded man inside the cabin. Miss, you go with them and show them where you want him. With your permission we'll rest up here till dawn.'

There was movement around her as men moved to carry out their orders, some tending to the horses, watering them and turning them loose in the corral while others carried her father inside the house. Gwendolyn went with them, worried they would hurt him as they manhandled him inside the house. She bent over her father in the bed and stared at his pale face.

'Julian Beam is a hoss doctor. If you want he'll take a look at him, see if he can do anything for him?'

Gwendolyn nodded her assent. A tall thin man, slightly stooped, moved up, tipping his hat to the girl.

'I'll do what I can for him, miss. Where did the bullet hit?'

'In his chest. It went through and I cut the bullet out of his back.' She was speaking with an effort to hold back the tears.

'That's good. He'll stand a better chance with no lead inside.'

'We got coffee, miss,' another man called, 'if you got some hot water.'

'Of course.'

She moved to the stove, stirred the embers to life and

pushed in more fuel. Still in a dream as if none of this had anything to do with her, she wondered if indeed it was a dream and these men were not real but she was still asleep outside by the well.

'Tom, fetch me the whiskey from my saddle-bag,' Julian called to one of his companions. 'An' don't be sneaking a drink on the sly. It's for medicinal purposes only.'

'You mean you been carrying whiskey with you and never asked a man if he had a mouth on him?'

'Just fetch the whiskey, Tom.'

Gwendolyn turned up the lamp and the room gradually took on a cosy glow as the flame brightened. The marshal studied her in the light and noted the cuts and bruises and pulped lips. She looked away ashamed under his gaze. The lawman was of a stocky build with stern eyes and several days' beard.

'We were following a trail we thought had gone cold. Ernest Jones and his gang robbed a bank and killed two people.' He made no reference to her battered face, guessing what had occurred without having to be told. 'Just you and your pa here, miss?'

She nodded. Tom came back in with the whiskey in one hand and a sack of coffee in the other. He handed the coffee to Gwendolyn and couldn't help staring at her messed-up face. She kept her head low and walked to the stove where the kettle was coming to the boil. The smell of the brew filled the small room, mixing with the man-smell of sweat and horse and tobacco that had come in with the visitors. Gwendolyn was kept busy serving up mugs of coffee. She remembered the sourdough bread she had made.

'There's some sourdough from yesterday,' she said.

'Sourdough, yes miss.'

The men voiced their approval of her offer. Gwendolyn began cutting the bread into thick slices.

26

'You done a good job on that bullet wound, miss.' Julian had come back in from the bedroom carrying the whiskey bottle. He held it out to Gwendolyn. 'Maybe after all you come through you could do with a slug of this whiskey in your coffee.'

'I . . . no . . . I don't think so.'

Gwendolyn had never tasted whiskey. Julian took Gwendolyn's mug and poured the liquor into the coffee.

'Believe me it will do you good. Help you sleep.'

She kept her eyes lowered and sipped the coffee with its strange medicinal taste.

'Thank you.'

'Miss, if you don't object we'll bed down here for the night. We won't be able to follow tracks till daylight. We'll talk about what you want to do in the morning. You go in and sit with your pa. We'll try not to be too much in the way.'

7

'Ben, where are you?'

Eliza Donohue looked from her companion to the still figure slumped on the floor, her eyes wide with fright.

'There's someone with him. What are we going to do?'

Brendon Prichard, general manager for the Donohue estates, was tall with dark good looks.

'Damn. There's only one thing to do.' Quickly he turned and gripped Eliza's blouse. 'Help me tear this. We'll tell that Truman tried to molest you and I had to rescue you.'

Under his fingers the blouse ripped down the front

exposing the twin mounds of her breasts.

'Remember, he attacked you. It's your word against his.'

'Goddamnit Ben, where the hell are you?'

'This way,' Brendon yelled. 'For God's sake hurry! Cover yourself,' he hissed, 'but not too much.'

Eliza looked down at her torn blouse and tugged at it. Around the corner of the house came Terry, still carrying the heart of flowers from the cemetery.

'Over here in the conservatory,' Brendon yelled. 'Hurry.'

Terry hastened into the glasshouse, his eyes drawn immediately to Eliza and her almost exposed breasts.

'Miss Eliza, what's going on?' Terry noticed the still form on the floor. 'Ben!'

He fell to his knee beside his friend and as he did so Ben groaned and stirred.

'Quick, help me secure him,' Brendon called urgently. 'There should be some rope about.'

'Rope? What are you talking about?'

'He attacked Miss Eliza. He was like a mad thing. I had to slug him with my pistol.'

'Attack? but. . . .' Terry spluttered, out of his depth. 'I don't understand.'

'Miss Eliza, tell him. Tell him what happened.'

'It's true,' There was a break in Eliza's voice. She looked down at her torn blouse and let it slip a little exposing delicate flesh. 'It was horrible.' She burst into tears. 'What am I going to tell Father?' she sobbed.

'Don't distress yourself, Miss Eliza,' Brendon stepped forward. 'Terry, you keep a watch on this swine while I fetch a rope. We'll truss him like the hog he is.'

Terry stood bewildered in the midst of this playacting, trying not to look at Eliza and the tantalizing glimpse of breasts exposed by the torn blouse but no matter how he tried his eyes strayed back.

'Ben – he was my best friend. I can't believe it.'

Eliza stopped sobbing long enough to cast a reproving glance at Terry.

'You saying I'm lying.'

And then Brendon was back with a coil of rope. Ben groaned and rolled on his back. Put his hand to his head and groaned again.

'Quick, lend a hand here afore he comes too. He was like a mad dog going at Miss Eliza like that.'

Reluctantly Terry helped.

'What the. . . ?' Ben was coming to his senses looking at the men roping his hands and feet, realizing what was happening and beginning to struggle but it was too late. The rope was secure. 'What the hell's going on? Why are you fellas doing this to me?'

Terry looked away unable to meet his friend's eye.

'You brute,' Brendon yelled, simulating anger. He backhanded the helpless Ben. 'What sort of monster are you, attacking a woman like that. You deserve to be horsewhipped and no doubt when Mr Donohue gets back he'll want to do it himself. If he doesn't, I sure will.' Another backhander rocked Ben's head.

'Hold on, Brendon. Quit hitting him. That's no way to treat a man tied up as he is.'

'After what he did! I feel like ripping his head off.'

'For God's sake tell me what the hell's going on,' Ben yelled. 'I come here with Terry and I end up getting the hell knocked out of me. Untie me, Prichard. Let's see how brave you are at hitting when I got my hands free.'

'Miss Eliza, you go in the house. Ain't no reason for you to see this cowardly monster more than is necessary.'

Eliza had been quietly sobbing while pulling at her ripped blouse exposing more than she was covering. Terry was torn between looking at the woman he professed he was madly in love with and staring with distaste at his erstwhile friend.

'Why'd you do it, Ben? I thought you were my friend.'

'Damnit, I ain't done nothing.' As Ben's head cleared he was beginning to put two and two together. 'Goddamnit, Prichard. This is a frame-up.' Ben was alternating glancing from his accuser to the distraught woman. 'Terry, can't you see what's happening? I caught them at it – your precious Miss Eliza and this—'

Ben got no further. Brendon Prichard's fist hit him full on the mouth.

'Shut your filthy mouth! How dare you accuse Miss Eliza of such a thing?'

Again Prichard's fist shot out. Blood poured freely from Ben's nose. He moaned and tried to roll away, but Prichard was merciless. Again and again he hit Ben. Ben twisted to get away from the punishment but his bonds kept him powerless to evade the brutal pounding.

'Hold on, Brendon.' Terry gripped Prichard's arm and tried to pull him away from Ben. 'It ain't right beating on him like that. No matter what he's done it just ain't right.'

Prichard turned an enraged face to Terry.

'Let go my arm, damn you. This fella's no better than an animal. I feel like taking out my shooter and putting an end to him here and now.'

They struggled for a time and while they were thus engaged Eliza made her escape back up to the big house leaving Prichard to carry on the charade meant to save her reputation and deflect the wrath of Pierce Donohue, her father, from her and her lover, Brendan Prichard.

Ben lay on the jailhouse bunk and stared through the iron bars of his cell. The man glaring balefully in at him was Pierce Donohue. He wore a Stetson and had a fat cigar jutting out of his mouth.

'Five years' hard labour in the penitentiary ain't no sentence for what you did to my daughter. You're an ungrateful dog! I gave you a job, paid your wages and what did you do? Like a mangy cur you turned on your benefactors and bit the hand that fed you.'

Slowly Ben slid from the bunk. He walked across to the bars of his cell and stared at the enraged face of the town boss.

'At the moment I am helpless inside this jail – put here by false testament,' he stated calmly. 'I've told the truth of what happened that night. One day the truth will out and I'll clear my name. Until that day comes I'd be thankful if you would leave me in peace.'

Donohue's face grew ugly with hatred as he glared at Ben.

'It sure was a blessing Brendon Prichard heard Eliza cry out and came to the rescue. He was my manager but I've promoted him to looking after Eliza. He's her personal bodyguard now.'

'Yeah, well I'm sure they'll make a lovely couple,' Ben said sardonically. 'I hope they get married and live happily ever after.'

'You swine!' Donohue's hands were clenching and unclenching as he stared impotently at the prisoner. 'Prichard has a wife back in Tucson. At least I know I have an honourable man looking after my daughter.'

Only the situation was so grim Ben wanted to laugh out loud at this news. Instead he turned his back on his tormentor and walked across to his bunk and lay down again. Donohue gripped the bars of the cell as if he was about to rip them from the sockets to get at the youngster lounging on the bunk but he had said all he wanted to say and he went back to the outer office leaving Ben alone once more to contemplate his fate. There came the jangling of keys and

Sheriff Bart Taylor appeared accompanied by his two deputies.

'Truman, get your lazy ass out of that bunk. It's vacation time for you. The governor of Sandell Penitentiary is anxiously awaiting you.'

Ben looked up.

'Sandell, hell I thought I was going to Anderson.'

The sheriff laughed harshly. 'Nah, nothing so easy. Mr Donohue is concerned for your welfare. He petitioned the governor to get you sent to Sandell.'

Ben slowly sat up. Everyone had heard of Sandell Penitentiary, the notorious top-security prison where the most dangerous lawbreakers were incarcerated. Ben, who was innocent of the crime of which he was accused, was to be caged with hardened criminals of the most brutal kind.

Gwendolyn did not sleep that night. She sat by her father's bedside numb with grief and fear. Her body ached from the abuse she had received at the hands of the outlaws but she ignored the discomfort, believing it to be a punishment for what had happened to her.

During the night she could hear men coughing, snoring or getting up to go outside. Occasionally one spoke in his sleep or she would hear the low murmur of voices as a wakeful man had a conversation with one of his companions.

During this long sleepless night Gwendolyn began to feel

revulsion at her weakness. A dread grew within her that her father might die and she would be left to cope all alone with the terrible shame of her ordeal.

Dry-eyed and numb she kept watch over her father till dawn skulked into the room via the small window that did not have glass but muslin tacked in place. The men in the next room stirred to life and still Gwendolyn sat by the side of her wounded father. The smell of coffee and the murmur of voices grew inside the house. Eventually a cautious head poked inside the doorway.

'Miss, we got coffee on the go. Julian wants to come in and see to your pa, if that's all right.'

'Thank you.'

When she tried to stand she found she had seized up and could not repress a small groan as her aches and pains surged to the fore.

'You all right, miss?' the voice anxious. 'You need any help?'

'No,' she croaked, 'I'll be all right.'

But she wasn't all right. Her body pained in every limb. To move was an agony. She got to her feet and like a woman with decades behind her shuffled to the door of the bedroom and passed through into the main room, which was all activity as men worked in the murky light of the dawn rolling up bedding and tidying after themselves. The front door opened and Tom walked in carrying saddle-bags.

'We got some fatback, miss,' he called. 'I'll get biscuits on and we'll have breakfast. Then we'll be out of your way.'

Gwendolyn nodded dumbly. Julian moved towards the bedroom.

'I'll take a look at your pa, miss. He should be a lot better after a peaceful night's rest. Did he awaken at all during the night?'

Gwendolyn shook her head, a feeling of faintness and

unreality overwhelming her. She just wanted to lie down somewhere quiet and be alone. The men in the room pretended not to watch her but she knew different. They were looking and thinking about what the gang did to her. She felt dirty and wanted to go out to the well and draw water and wash. But she knew she could not do that while the posse remained so she endured, answering any queries or remarks put to her in monosyllables, her face not showing any expression and not looking directly at the men in the room. Julian, the horse doctor came back from the bedroom.

'Miss, I think your pa needs medical treatment more than I can give him. I'm all right with horses but humans are different.'

She felt a stab of dread at his words.

'We'll be going on after those outlaws when we've ate, miss. First town we come to, we'll send a sawbones out to tend your pa. If your pa comes to, try and get him to drink something.'

The smell of frying fatback mingled with the tang of coffee in the small house. A plate was handed to Gwendolyn but she was not hungry and after gazing at the food she put the plate by and went back to the bedroom to sit with her father. With her exit the activity and noise increased in the main room as the men ate their breakfast and discussed plans for the day.

'Those varmints will be heading for Drygulch Canyon. Once in there we'll never get them. We'll need to push on hard today if we stand a chance of catching up.'

'According to the gal they lit out afore sundown yesterday. If they hole up for the night like we did here, there's a chance we'll maybe catch up with them.'

Gwendolyn listened to their chatter and wanted to tell the men to stop talking and eating and go after the brutes that had shot her father. She stared at the wounded man, noting the marble-like face, devoid of colour, so unlike the kindly active man she was so fond of. Julian came inside. He was carrying the whiskey bottle now half empty.

'Miss, I'm leaving this here whiskey for you. You might want to wash the wound again.'

She looked at the bottle, not wanting to look at his eyes and see the pity in them. Julian set the bottle on the cabinet.

'Thank you.' Her voice was faint, without emotion.

'We're all sorry about what happened. The boys, they had a collection.' He placed a handful of coins and banknotes on the bed. 'It's for the sawbones when he comes, miss. We'll send him back here and tell him you have money to pay.'

Gwendolyn stared at the crumpled notes and coins on the bed. She knew she should say something – try and thank these rough kindly men who chased outlaws. There were no words. She could only nod – sit with bowed head, too numb to think of anything but her father lying so pale and still in the bed.

Julian raised his hand as if to pat her head . . . wanting to comfort this poor damaged girl, hesitated and let his hand fall to his side.

'Miss. . . .'

She heard him leave, listening to the shuffle of boots as men vacated the house and the murmur of voices outside as they saddled up. There was the sound of hoof beats as they departed, the reverberation lingering, then fading as they went further and further out into the prairie in their hunt for Ernest Jones and his gang of killers.

She was alone again with her injured father lying on the bed hovering between life and death.

9

The posse rode hard. Well rested after the night spent at the cabin where they found the dying farmer and his abused daughter, they made good progress in pursuit of the outlaw gang.

At midday they called a halt to give the horses a rest and a mouthful of water. They had refreshed their canteens at the farm but drank sparingly not quite knowing when the next waterhole would be available.

'If we don't catch up on them varmints afore they get to Drygulch Canyon we may kiss them goodbye,' ventured Marshal Quigley. 'Once they're in those rocks we'll never winkle them out.'

'Harold, I reckon you're right,' Julian Beam opined. 'That hellhole is a nest of rattlers. Leastways I'd rather wade in amongst rattlers than tangle with a mess of gunnies from that Dryguch Canyon.'

'I keep thinking of that poor gal back at that farm. What are the chances for her pa? You reckon he'll make it?'

'Hell I know. Some of these sodbusters are tougher than your ordinary townsfolk. They have to be to survive out here. But to tell the truth I wouldn't give a bent nickel for his chances. I reckon he's bleeding internally and there's not a lot can be done for that.'

'Son of a bitch. I bet they just shot him for the hell of it. An' that poor girl, they abused her some, too.'

'Yeah, she was keeping it bottled up, poor thing. But she's young and she's tough. I reckon she'll pull through.'

'When we come upon her like that unawares, we sure

spooked her. Reckon she thought Jones and his gang had come back.'

'Yeah, poor kid. OK, mount up. We'll go on. Tom reckons the next waterhole is the last one afore Drygulch Canyon. Jones will most likely stop there afore heading for his hideout. My thinking is, if we push on hard now we might just happen upon them varmints. They won't be expecting us to chase them this far. We might just be lucky and catch up with them.'

'I don't know, Marshal. Jones is as cunning as a coyote. That's why he's run free for so long. He ain't going to be caught napping.'

'Julian, if we all thought like that nothing would ever get done. What do you suggest; we all turn our horses and go on back? I ain't come this far to give up that easy.'

With a tired and despondent posse riding behind him, Marshal Quigley pushed on in pursuit of the wily bandit, Ernest Jones.

The waterhole the posse was heading for was about five miles further in the direction they were heading. At that moment it was occupied. Ernest Jones and his crew had spent the night there and were lazily thinking of rousing themselves and pushing on towards the hideout in the hills.

'Riders, boss,' the lookout called.

'Looks like a sizeable bunch,' Jones opined as he stared out at the oncoming riders. 'They're coming from the wrong direction to be that posse that was chasing us. It's too late to make a run for it. They'll catch us out in the open. Tell everyone to keep their weapons handy till we know if they're friendly.'

The dozen or so riders came on at an easy lope towards the waterhole. Jones stepped out in full view of the new-comers and waved a greeting. His men were in the trees with guns drawn watching for any sign of hostility.

'Howdy, fellas. We were just leaving. The water's all yours free for the asking.'

'What the hell you mean, free?' the leading rider growled. 'I take what I want when I wants.'

'Beniah Arnold, I'll be damned. You sure don't get no less ornery.'

'Son of a bitch, Ernest Jones by God, I thought you'd be dead by now.'

The riders pulled into the space by the waterhole and began to dismount.

'What the hell are you doing here, Beniah? Last I heard you were over in Kansas kicking up a storm.'

The two men stood together and grasped hands. Arnold was stockily built with broad shoulders and blunt features.

'Things got a mite hot down there. Texas Rangers after my hide. Thought I'd come over here an' lie low till things calm down a mite. Someone told us about a place called Drygulch Canyon where a fella could bed down and not be bothered too much by the law.'

'Beniah, you sure fell in lucky. That's where me and the boys are heading. You sure welcome to join us. Drygulch is a prospering town filled with every jack villain under the sun. No lawman dare come within ten mile of the place.'

'Ernest, I reckon I'd as soon bed down with a little ole grizzly as shack up with you and your kin,' Arnold said, taking the sting out of his remark with a grin. 'But beggars can't be choosers. My men and I need a breather. Give us time to grab a bite to eat and a drink an' we'll tag along just to keep your ass out of trouble.'

'It's been a while since you and I were together, Beniah. I'll buy you a drink back in Drygulch and we can chaw the fat some over old times.'

While the leaders of their respective gangs were chatting, their men were getting acquainted. Some of them knew each other from times past when they had raided together. There was much banter and ribald humour as the newcomers busied themselves watering their horses and filling canteens.

'You fellas got anything to eat?'

'Sure, we got a few beans and coffee and jerky. You want a brew up?'

'Goddamnit, our food ran out a couple of days ago. I was near eating my tobacco pouch I was that hungry.'

'Ernest, we got time to feed these fellas afore we light out?'

'Sure, but hurry it up. We want to be at Drygulch Canyon afore sunset. Those fellas guarding the pass get itchy trigger fingers come nightfall.'

'Break out them beans. You can be supping them while we get the coffee going. There's still a spark in that there fire. Could do with another drink myself. Mind you, when we get to Drygulch Canyon I reckon I ain't going to drink nothing but bourbon for a week.'

The grove where the waterhole was situated was alive with noise and activity as men chatted and ate what spare food was available. So occupied were the outlaws they lingered longer than was wise and paid the price of their dilatoriness.

'Riders coming, Ernest.'

'What in tarnation!'

The two outlaw chiefs peered out at the dust cloud in the distance. Jones took a glass from his pocket and studied the riders.

'It's that goddamn posse. Who'd have thought they'd still be on our trail.' He folded the glass and turned back to the men gathered amongst the trees. 'Saddle up boys; we got some riding ahead of us.'

'How many you reckon?' Arnold asked peering into the distance.

'Six, I counted. Why you ask?'

Beniah Arnold turned and looked at his old riding partner. There was an evil glint in his eyes.

'There are fifteen of us.'

'What're you suggesting?'

'Why run when you can stand and fight? The odds are on our side. We could stop that posse once and for all.'

10

'There she lays – Little Buffalo waterhole – the last water between here and Drygulch Canyon.'

Sheriff Quigley nodded. 'Sure a welcome sight. Those trees will give a bit of shade. We'll have a break here and restock our water afore deciding how much further we want to go.'

While this conversation was going on the posse was getting closer to the waterhole. The horses, smelling the water, were pulling impatiently, eagerly increasing their pace. Sheriff Quigley was pulling on his reins.

'Whoa, you damn jughead.'

The horse did not want to stop and fought the bridle, thirst being more pressing than the wishes of the rider. Then something occurred that changed the whole course of events. It was as straightforward as a rattlesnake on the same path as the posse. The snake sent out a warning rattle as the horses trod too close.

'Damn!'

Marshal Quigley heaved on his reins but the horse was

thoroughly spooked. With its ears back, it took off at a gallop.

'Hell, Sheriff, no need to rush. There'll be enough for all of us.'

'Whoopee!'

The posse dug in heels and followed their leader. After days of trailing the outlaws the men were jaded and discouraged. The sight of the sheriff impotently pulling on the reins of his spooked mount was a rare moment of entertainment. Yelling and whooping, the riders surged after the sheriff.

'Last man in buys the drinks!'

It descended into a race with Sheriff Quigley in the lead and likely to win. The men concealed at the waterhole watched in some bemusement as the posse raced towards them.

'Damn fellas must be kind of thirsty.'

'Sure seems that way.'

'I hope they're hungry. I got me a barrel of lead to pour in their bellies.'

'Come and get it!'

'Let them get right in afore you start shooting. We want them all.'

It was too easy. The posse hurtled towards the trees that marked the waterhole – trees that hid fifteen heavily armed men. The outlaws watched the riders rush towards the death awaiting for them, and licked their lips in anticipation, readied their weapons.

Fifty yards from the trees and Ernest Jones put a rifle bullet square into Sheriff Quigley. It was the signal for a barrage of lead to pour out from the grove. Horses were hit. Riders were hit. Men tried to haul their mounts around to stop the headlong dash. In some cases not even lead bullets halted the onward impetus.

The horses ploughed on, made more panicked by the

screaming of wounded beasts around them, some going down on their knees and throwing their riders. One or two riders flung themselves from the bolting mounts and tumbled to the ground then scrambled to shelter behind downed animals and comrades. There was no other cover.

They pulled pistols or managed to drag rifles from scabbards as they crouched behind the carcasses of their mounts. And all the while the deadly barrage of lead hammered into the dead and living both.

Sheriff Quigley lay in the dirt unable to move. The shot that had come so unexpectedly out of the trees had hit him in the chest, smashing his breast bone and stunning him. He struggled to breathe through the pain, trying to understand what had happened but blackness crept down across his vision and he drifted into darkness. He did not witness the annihilation of his band of deputies.

The torrent of lead never slackened even when there was no return fire from the stricken posse. At last the firing petered out as the guns grew hot and the outlaws ran low on ammunition.

'Goddamnit.'

Ernest Jones stood upright and looked at the bloody scene stretched out in the sands. All around him men emerged from behind trees and stood and gazed in admiration at their work.

'Whoopee!' someone yelled. 'That was the best bit of shooting I've had in a coon's age.'

'Yippee! It sure beats shooting rocks an' cans.'

'You reckon they're all dead?'

'Anyone as survives that lead storm ought to get a medal.'

'Sure thing, an' a certificate to go with it.'

'Writ on his tombstone.'

Hardly believing what they had done the outlaws were venturing out of the trees for a closer view of the carnage.

They still carried weapons at the ready just in case there were survivors.

Horses and men lay scattered indiscriminately in the dirt, limbs sprawled lifelessly. There was a movement to one side and swiftly a dozen guns swung in that direction. A wounded horse had lifted its head from the dirt and whinnied feebly. The outlaws ignored the cries of distress and continued to examine their handiwork.

'Have a look around. Make sure there are no survivors.'

'Hell, does it matter if anyone survives this? They ain't going anywhere. No mounts and full of lead.'

'Yeah, I guess you're right. Search their pockets see if anyone got any valuables.'

'Damnit, leave them as they lie. Ain't right to rob the dead. That doesn't sit right with me. It'll bring nothing but bad luck.'

'Yeah, maybe you're right. OK, fellas, mount up and let's get the hell out of here. Leave this lot for the buzzards.'

11

Gwendolyn stood in the yard with a feeling of loneliness like a vacant pit inside. Tears were flowing freely as she stared out into the distance, not seeing anything. There was a movement to one side and she twisted quickly, fear stabbing like a knife. The solemn face of the mule was quietly regarding her.

'Oh, you did give me a start.'

When she spoke the mule shambled the few steps to meet

her and Gwendolyn put her hand out, feeling the rough hair. The large head moved up and down under her caress. Impulsively she put her arms around the mule's neck and hugged tightly. She hung there on the mule and somehow it was a comfort that there was another creature to share her grief.

'Pa is dead,' she said. 'He needs to be buried. I don't think I have the strength to do that.'

As she looked at the house she had a sudden urge to leave. She could no longer bear to live on here with the terrible memories the place held. As she stood in the yard the place no longer felt like home. A reckless notion to destroy the house and with it all the ugly memories within swept over her.

Her mind made up, she began her preparations. She went back inside and packed a few items of clothing along with blankets and some trinkets that had belonged to her mother. The knife and the ancient rifle went too. All the time she worked, she was conscious of the body of her dead father lying so still in the bedroom. Taking her pathetic bundle outside Gwendolyn contemplated her next move. She knew what she wanted to do. She just wasn't sure how to accomplish it.

The tools were kept in an outhouse and Gwendolyn fetched the spade. With no one but the mule to watch, Gwendolyn started near the door. Working steadily she punched a hole in the wall. As the dwelling was made of sods it was easy going. Threading a rope through the hole and back out through the door she tied the end to the mule's harness.

Gwendolyn urged the mule forward. Slowly the animal took up the strain leaning into the harness. Nothing happened and Gwendolyn added her weight to the rope. There was a dull ripping sound and the door frame moved.

'Keep pulling,' she yelled.

The doorframe twisted and suddenly came free, falling out into the yard. With that support gone the front of the house drooped and the roof sagged. There was no stopping the slow disintegration as roof beams gave way collapsing inwards, giving up clouds of dust as the dried sods crumbled. Gwendolyn watched without emotion at the destruction she had wrought. When the dust had settled she stood for a moment in silent prayer.

'Goodbye, Pa. This was your house and I think it fitting for you to remain at peace here. Life was hard for us both. I reckon it was hard for Ma as well. Now you are together in a better place.'

Gwendolyn had been born here and now she was preparing to venture out into a world of which she was largely ignorant.

She fashioned a serviceable saddle using the blankets she had retrieved from the house and lashed this atop the mule. Her bundle of possessions were rolled into a sausage and tied on the front. Then she made a pouch for the rifle out of her father's oil coats and attached this to the roll. She practiced getting the weapon in and out of its holding place. The knife she stuck in her belt. With one last look at the tomb she had created for her dead father, Gwendolyn climbed aboard the mule and gathered the rope bridle.

'I figure the way to go is in the same direction as that posse,' she mused. 'Mayhap we can join up with them and that way it'll be safer than trying to make it on my own. But no man will ever lay hands on me again. If that happens either he will die or I will die or maybe both.'

Gwendolyn jigged the reins and clapped her heels into the mule's side and moving out, followed the tracks made by the posse.

As night fell so too did Gwendolyn's spirits. She had

travelled all day without sighting another living being. Hills loomed on the horizon and it was in that direction the tracks she was following were heading. She picked a dip in the land that gave slight protection from the stiff wind and, gathering a few twigs and buffalo chips, she got a fire going. She brewed coffee but did not feel like eating.

Left to fend for itself, the mule foraged for grass and anything else edible. Gwendolyn huddled by the fire listening to the soft noises of the mule. She had the unreal feeling that other than the mule she was the only living person left in the world. Staring up at the star-filled sky she had the conviction she was a minute speck in the immensity of the universe.

'I am a thing without size or substance. God has abandoned me. I will wander this wilderness and never find what I am looking for. And what am I looking for? Even I don't know what that is. So even if I do find it I will not know that I have found it for I am unaware of the object of the search.' These thoughts made her head ache and she rubbed her forehead. 'Perhaps that is my destiny. I shall wander the earth without purpose. But what was I before today? I was a farmer's daughter. Every day was a struggle to make things grow. I never thought much further than the next task or the next day. When the rain did not come in time our crops were stunted and we struggled to survive. Mother gave up and passed on and now Father is with her. They belong together whilst I belong to no one. I am a soiled creature. I am not fit for the company of men.'

In the end, tiredness overcame her and crawling into the blankets she fell, eventually, into an exhausted sleep. It was not a restful sleep. Dark shapes stalked her dreams and though she fled through the night she could not evade their frightening advances or their ghastly activities.

Gwendolyn awoke in the dawn, gritty-eyed and fatigued. Desultorily she got a fire going and made hot coffee. Faint hunger pains stirred her to cook a breakfast of fatback and biscuits. In the end she did not finish the meal and stored the leftovers for another time.

Packing up camp did not take long and Gwendolyn set out once more on the well-marked trail of the posse. As the sun rose higher in the sky so too did the temperature. Nothing stirred on the horizon. She was in no hurry, which was just as well for the mule had only one speed: a steady plod.

As she rode she kept a sharp lookout and occasionally would put her hand on the rifle butt jutting from her home-made sling. She practiced pulling the weapon and putting a bullet in the breech till she was satisfied she would be armed and ready if danger threatened. Gwendolyn knew she could trust no one.

At midday she took a break, sipping her water and staring out at the imprecise shape of the hills towards which she was heading. At that moment she could hear no sound. It was as if she was the only person left in the world. Her isolation was a physical lump inside her.

All around her the heat of the air and the silence of the land and the emptiness of the distance squeezed her like a giant hand holding her in its grip. It was a sunburned waste-land she looked out on and her loneliness was that of an abandoned child.

She rose and walked over to the mule. It lifted its head and looked at her with its large liquid eyes. She felt she had to hold on to something alive – something physical – before this lonely feeling swallowed her. The mule waited expectantly anticipating a morsel of food. Gwendolyn pressed her face against the mule's head feeling the coarse hair against her cheek. It was with a supreme effort of will that she let go of the animal and contemplated what she had to do.

'I must follow the posse. Perhaps with them I can make

my way to some town and lose myself.'

But in truth she did not know what she wanted. The future was a blank and she felt she was sleepwalking into a nameless and unforeseen way of life. She was treading on sand and with every step she took towards that future the past closed up behind her and if she looked back there was nothing to see.

12

Sandell Penitentiary was one of the older institutions, built in the early part of the century. Thick adobe walls, baked under a relentless sun for decades, looked like they had been standing since the beginning of time. Hardened criminals were incarcerated there for it had a reputation of breaking the most stubborn and rebellious of men. To this infamous establishment came Ben Truman in the company of thirteen other felons.

Hard-faced, rifle-carrying warders welcomed the new inmates with both physical and verbal abuse.

'You are scum!'

'Mangy dogs!'

'Scabby animals!'

These and other epithets were yelled at the prisoners. And to emphasize the powerlessness of the newcomers the brutal warders hit out indiscriminately with rifle butts. Ben was hit on the shoulder and his arm went numb with the force of the blow. He, along with his fellow prisoners, scrambled to get out of the way but the warders were set on teaching this new intake a lesson.

The prisoners had arrived in hell and their keepers' job was to torment them. From now on they would leap to attention and jump instantly to do as ordered. Slowness in moving would be rewarded with a rifle butt and often commands would be emphasized with blows just for the hell of it. Evidently enjoying their task the guards kicked and punched the prisoners into some sort of line-up.

'Stand to attention, you feeble pieces of shit. In a while Governor Adamson will address you. You much as twitch while he's talking, your spine will be broken and you'll be staked out for the buzzards.'

The speaker was a bull of a man with the face of a pugilist that had fought too many fights. His nose was squashed flat, his eyebrows had swollen beyond their normal size and one ear was missing.

The prisoners stood in the hot sun and sweated and thirsted and waited for Governor Adamson. The guards retreated to the comparative shade of the prison wall and fashioned smokes while they idled and kept a beady eye on their victims.

Clean shaven with a cadaverous face on which a perpetual scowl was etched, Governor Adamson made his entrance. He wore a white Stetson and suit with shirt and string tie.

'The only way out of here for you scum is into a hole in the ground,' he growled.

Still smarting from the undeserved blow to his shoulder, Ben stared fascinated at the man who held the power of life and death over them. To Ben those hooded eyes reminded him of a vulture's.

'At all times you will address your guards as "sir". You move when told to. You stop when told. You never speak without permission. You sleep when I allow it. You work. You work hard. Slackers will be disciplined. All infringements of the rules will be punished severely. I will tell you the methods we use to discipline disobedience. There is the coffin.'

At he spoke Governor Adamson pointed to a rough wooden box that stood upright within the prison yard. It was indeed shaped like a coffin. All heads turned to look.

'Did I give you permission to move?' the governor barked. 'Guards!'

The guards came away from the shade of the wall like a swarm of rodents and descended upon the luckless prisoners. They used their rifles as clubs to hit the hapless men in the yard. Flailing left and right they waded in and beat the men into the dirt.

Prisoners flinched and tried to cower away but it was useless. There was nowhere to go. The guards were sadists, used to beating helpless men and their enjoyment was plain to see as they set to their task with unwarranted enthusiasm.

Ben received a savage blow on the head that felled him. As he lay dazed, a boot in the ribs jerked him into action. Instinctively he grabbed the foot and twisted hard. It was enough to unbalance the guard and the man went down. His face twisted into hatred as the guard scrambled to his feet. Ben was, at the same time, trying to get upright. The rifle butt hit him in the spine.

'Aaaah!'

Ben arched his back and the rifle cracked into his head. It was hard enough to put him in the dirt once more. Another boot almost lifted him into the air again. Ben was spared further punishment when the governor called for order.

'Enough!'

His men, savage and brutal they might be, were conditioned to obedience. Discipline was harsh amongst them. It had to be, for some were ex-convicts recruited purely because of their brutal natures. The beating stopped and the guards slowly retreated, glaring hatred at the bruised and bleeding prisoners.

'Stand to attention!' the governor shouted.

The beaten men slowly shuffled together in an attempt to stand in an orderly manner. Some had to be helped upright. Ben was one of them.

'Get up,' someone hissed in his ear. 'You got to get up.'

Ben made it upright and stood swaying, his body screaming in protest. Ribs, back, head – all ached intolerably and Ben was sick and dizzy. It was with a supreme effort of will he managed to remain erect.

'I see you are a stubborn and rebellious batch of gophers. You obviously didn't take in what I said at the start. You move when told to and only then. You have no initiative of your own. You are entirely under my control. Is that clear?'

The row of men stood bowed and beaten. No one responded.

'Guards!'

The guards swarmed forward eager for the second assault. Their victims cowered back, arms raised for protection, bodies bent to present a smaller target. The guard that tangled with Ben on the first attack went for him again. Blows rained down on the helpless men and Ben was savagely beaten to the dirt.

'Enough!'

Once more the command rang out and reluctantly the brutal guards retreated. By this time, Ben was barely conscious and was held upright by his neighbour, a lanky, bearded man with narrow face, deeply gouged with a knife scar.

'When I ask a question I expect an answer. I asked you a question and stubbornly you refused to answer. We shall try again and see if you are still determined to maintain this obstinacy. Is that clear?'

A few mumbled assent while some were merely capable of nodding. Others like Ben were too dazed to follow the drift of the governor's talk.

'Is that the best you can do? Guards!'

The harsh lessons continued till there was not a man among the prisoners capable of standing.

At noon when the sun stood at its hottest Governor Adamson went for his lunch. The new intake of prisoners sprawled in the yard, bruised bloody and thoroughly cowed.

13

'Hell, you can write?'

'Yeah.' Ben was surprised at the question. 'Sure I can write. I can read and write. Why you ask?'

William Douglas squinted back at Ben. 'Hell, you can write. Ain't that something.'

Douglas was a lean cadaver of a man with a mean, knife-scarred face. For reasons unknown to Ben the unsavoury-looking character had befriended the youngster. During that first day of violent initiation Douglas had reached out a helping hand. Alone and bewildered by his sudden descent into the brutal regime of prison Ben had reason to be grateful for the friendship of this sinister-looking man.

They were a strange pair, this battle-scarred man and Ben Truman, but the pairing had worked in Ben's favour. The more brutal prisoners who had looked upon the youthful

Ben as easy meat were wary of Douglas for he had a reputation that preceded him into the prison.

'What you in for, William?' Ben had asked in the early part of their friendship.

'Robbing banks.' When Ben started to laugh Douglas looked at him sourly. 'What's so funny about robbing banks?

'I was a security guard for a bank. You ever rob a bank in Downsville?'

'Downsville.' Douglas squinted into the distance. 'Don't recollect that one. Would it be worth a try, you think?'

Ben thought of joining up with William Douglas to rob Pierce Donohue's bank.

'If I ever get out of here I might just ask for some advice on robbing banks. That's one bank I would like to hit.'

Douglas was watching Ben closely. 'You reckon there's big money in this Downsville?'

'Hell, I don't know. It's just the thought of getting back at the man who put me in this place.'

'You say you were a security guard; that mean you were caught stealing from the bank?'

'No, I never took a penny except my wages which was due.' Ben sighed and looked at the ground. 'I never imagined I would end up in prison for something I never did.'

They were in a cell crowded to capacity. Twelve men shared the one small area. Privacy was non-existent. Private conversations were impossible unless the inmates stuck their mouth against an ear and whispered. But no one cared enough to do that.

'Everyone says that,' a pock-faced man on the other side of Douglas remarked. 'We're all innocent in here, ain't we fellas?'

There were grunts of acknowledgement along with a few sniggers.

'Yeah, well when a fella catches the boss's manager

banging the daughter of the bank owner he walks into an ambush.'

There was a stir of interest around the cell as heads came up at the hint of a juicy story.

'Tell us fella. What happened?'

'What was she like, the banker's daughter? Was she a looker?'

'Did you get a piece of the action?'

'What was she wearing?'

Prisoners were shifting and agitated as they tried to get nearer to the youngster who claimed he had witnessed a banker's daughter being topped. Ben was not comfortable having to relive the experiences that had led to his incarceration. He tried to defuse the situation that was developing.

'Hell, I was just in the wrong place at the wrong time. I saw nothing. Only the banker's daughter and her boyfriend thought I did. That's all. They decided to get me out of the way just in case I blabbed off about it.'

'Hell damnit boy, you mean you saw nothing; didn't see her take her clothes off or see her naked or nothing?'

'Nope. The bit as sticks in my craw is if I had seen them at it I wouldn't have said a damn thing about it. The way I figured it was none of my business and I'd have walked away from it and let them get on with it. I ain't one to give out tittle-tattle about what people do.'

'The hell with that,' Douglas broke in. 'What I was asking about was you could write.'

'Why you want to know for?'

'Cos I reckon there's someone I need to write to – let him know where I am at.'

'Why can't you write yourself?'

'Cos numskull, I can't write.'

'Oh, I see. Yeah, well . . . yeah. . . .' Ben stumbled to a halt not knowing how to handle this disclosure. 'OK, that's OK.

I'll write it for you . . . write what you want.'

'I got to ask the governor and if he says yeah, then the screws will give us paper and stuff to write the letter.'

'You have to ask?'

'This is a prison, don't forget. If the governor allows, the screws have to be bribed to let you have the writing things.'

'Bribed! Goddamnit. We don't have no rights at all in here.'

'I keep telling you, it's a goddamn prison for gawd's sake.'

It took nearly a week for the negotiations to be completed and Douglas presented Ben with a creased and dirty piece of paper and a stub of a pencil.

'Huh, you don't get much for your tobacco,' Ben complained as he contemplated the grubby articles he had to work with.

'Just you write what I tell you,' Douglas said and began to dictate. 'Dear Janis, they got me banged up in Sandell. Tell cousin Ernest where I am at. Tell him I'm sorry I'm not there to help with the roundup. I wish I was there now instead of in prison. I hope to see you soon. William Douglas.'

Ben finished writing and looked up at William.

'That it?'

'Yeah, that's it. Kin I see it?'

Ben handed over the completed note. The scar-faced man held the paper tenderly as if it were something fragile and easily damaged while he scrutinized the contents.

'You reckon this is all right?' he asked at last.

'Sure, it's a good letter. You want to make your mark or something?'

'Yeah, I can make my mark,' Douglas replied, and laboriously scribed X on the bottom of his letter.

'Is Janis your wife?'

'Nah, she's like a bosom friend.'

'What address you want?'

'The Silver Nugget, Pipersville.'

'Janis got a second name?'

'Janis Corbin.'

There was a rustle of activity and a piece of paper was pushed in front of Ben's face.

'Wha—' Ben looked up surprised.

'Write me letter, Ben Truman.' There was no threat in the brutal face of Issachar Roberts, just an intense look of mortification at having to ask another man for assistance. The bruiser stared down at the paper he was holding out towards Ben. 'You write?' It was not a demand but a request.

Slowly Ben reached out and took the proffered paper.

'What you want me to write?'

There was deathly hush within the crowded cell and as Ben waited for a reply he noted with surprise the number of men staring anxiously at him. As far as he could make out they all had scraps of dog-eared paper clutched in their fists.

14

Gwendolyn saw the buzzards as she sat atop her mule, watching them with feelings of revulsion, remembering her own frightening encounter with the winged scavengers. Lazily they hovered in the air currents and one by one, languidly dropped out of sight.

'Some poor beast at their mercy.'

There was so many of the evil birds she surmised there had been a lot of killing. Maybe a herd of buffalo or cattle had been caught in some mishap. She noted with unease her own trajectory was taking her directly towards the site of the birds' activity. Gwendolyn shuddered involuntarily then reached out and touched the wooden stock of her rifle.

'At least I got a weapon to fend off any trouble,' she muttered.

The mule plodded steadily on, seemingly tireless in its stately progress towards the distant hills. Gwendolyn thought of how she would present herself to the lawmen.

'They'll probably say they don't want to be saddled with no female. Well I can ride and I can shoot.'

Even though she did not relish spending time with the lawmen she was aware of a feeling of vulnerability out in the wilderness on her own. It was enough to keep her vigilant, with her hand straying often to the reassuring feel of the rifle tucked into her baggage.

Making her way towards the trees, always with an eye on the well-marked trail she came at the place where the buzzards were feeding. The mule stopped abruptly, even reversed a step, then stood trembling.

Gwendolyn stared aghast at the gruesome scene before her; the occasional flapping of powerful wings, the heads ducking as they plunged powerful beaks into flesh. The eyes were always first to go, the soft succulent flesh easily plundered. Men and horses were strewn where they had fallen; a ghastly banquet of flesh for the deadly predators now gorging on this unexpected and abundant feast.

'Ooooh. . . .'

She gripped the reins and her first impulse was to turn and flee from this horrific scene. There was obviously nothing she could do to help these poor souls lying unburied. And then she heard a horse squealing. Somewhere among that blood fest was an animal being eaten alive.

For long moments Gwendolyn hung there in the act of

fleeing from this nightmare of blood and gore and ripped flesh. The horse whinnied again, the sound like an arrow piercing her heart. Impulsively she pulled her rifle and aimed it into the swarming blood-soaked scavengers.

She began firing, pumping bullets at the feathered mass of heaving birds. The air seemed to stir around her like the pressure from a coming thunderstorm as frantic buzzards took to wing. A horrible cawing of raucous protests broke like a wave over her and she trembled with fright.

Gwendolyn kneed her mount forward. Reluctantly the animal stepped out, hesitant. She stopped firing and instead began yelling and waving her weapon in the air as they went forward towards that hovering mass of cruel heads and beady eyes and flapping wings.

She tried not to look at the eviscerated bodies spread out like the contents of a vast abattoir. Sightless eye sockets stared out at nothing; horses lay with their bellies torn open and intestines ripped out to fester in the harsh sun. Men's faces were eaten away or pieces had been gouged out with powerful pincer-like beaks. The smell hit like a swarm of tiny insects crawling into her nasal cavities causing her to cough and choke. Her eyes misted over and hot tears spilled.

'Goddamn you all to hell,' she cried in uncharacteristic language.

Gwendolyn did not know where the words came from but it seemed appropriate to use them in this extreme situation. Gwendolyn slowly advanced, the air above the corpses black with circling birds as they hung around reluctant to abandon their gory banquet.

Gwendolyn stopped at the edge of the bloody remains. The smell, the sights, the malignant birds hovering overhead all combined to break her self-control and she hung over the side of the mule and vomited. And all the while the strident protest from overhead went on relentlessly.

Gwendolyn recovered her upright position on the mule. Her eyes were misted with tears and her head ached and she had a foul taste in her mouth. She wanted to wrench the mule's head around and ride away. But through the raucous complaints from the frustrated buzzards came the shrill whinnies of an animal in distress. Biting her lip Gwendolyn urged the mule forward but it did not move. Gwendolyn kicked her heels into her mount's ribs. But the mule stayed rooted to the spot.

'Goddamnit, what's the matter?'

But no amount of urging on her part could induce the mule to go forward.

'You're spooked, old fella. Well I don't blame you. I'm sure spooked myself but I can't just ride away. I got to help those poor horses even if it's only to put them out of their misery.'

She slid from the mule and stared out across the field of blood trying not to focus on the broken bodies strewn in attitudes of death along with their mounts. With that came the sudden recognition that she knew these men. Only yesterday she had spoken and drank coffee with them. A hand squeezed her heart and she felt faint. Who had done this terrible deed?

Slowly she forced herself to step forward. Some of the buzzards had landed again while she had been preoccupied with the mule. Her anger snapped and she fired at the birds. There was wild screeching and an agitated surge as the birds took flight. She noted with satisfaction one of the carrion birds stayed on the ground, evidence of her accurate shooting. The flock of buzzards lifted higher into the air, taking the clamour of their angry squawking with them.

'Thank God for that,' she muttered and hesitantly stepped forward.

The noise was faint and indefinite. Gwendolyn frowned

and paused. Somewhere to her left the sound came again. Gwendolyn stayed quite still not sure if her senses were deceiving her. The slight sound whispered out again from the field of death.

'Help me.'

High overhead the buzzards circled, hovering, hungering to get back to their feasting.

'Help. . . .' The sound like the softest sigh.

Gwendolyn stood so still she might have become a tombstone for the corpses of the men strewn about the bloody ground.

'Am I going mad?' she whispered. 'I am hearing voices now.'

She could not move; had no will to do anything other than stand motionless. And she was frightened.

The horse that had been whinnying in pain called out once more, the cry much weaker. Forcing her feet to move Gwendolyn paced slowly forward. She knew what had to be done but it was not easy to walk through that field of blood. Her eyes, her nose all her senses were assaulted by the sights and sounds of that dreadful carnage. It took all her resolution to go on. She stopped by the horse, a piebald, its flanks heaving, its eye sockets brutally empty.

'Rest in peace,' she murmured as she placed the rifle behind its ear.

She closed her eyes as she pulled the trigger. Trembling she turned to leave when that whisper of sound came again. Like a sigh without enunciation.

In the midst of that terrible carnage Gwendolyn stood petrified. She closed her eyes but opened them immediately, more fearful of what she could not see than what she could see in front of her. Gradually she forced herself to look at the bodies of the men. A whimper of anguish broke from her. In amongst the dead was a man still with breath in him enough to call for help.

'I'm here. Hang on,' she cried and stumbled towards the place she thought the plea for help came.

15

Marshal Quigley was lying beside his dead horse. His eyes fluttered open and he stared up at the shape looming above him. Blood saturated his shirt. His face was drained of colour and he looked like one of the corpses amongst which he lay. Gwendolyn dropped to her knees beside him.

'Marshal Quigley.'

'They're dead, aren't they?' he whispered.

Gwendolyn nodded. She felt helpless as she stared at the bloody shirt. The nightmare was happening once more and she saw again her father sprawled by the well with Ernest Jones's bullet in his chest.

'I . . . I'll get some water . . . wash your wound.'

She made to get up again but Quigley raised a hand.

'Don't go. I ain't got much time.' He squinted up at her. 'You're the kid from the farm. What're you doing out here?' He gasped out the words, every breath laborious.

'My pa, he died. I . . . I followed you . . . didn't know what else to do.'

Quigley closed his eyes and Gwendolyn thought for a moment the lawman had passed away.

'Poor kid. Gwendolyn, isn't it?'

'Yes,' she whispered. 'What can I do for you?'

She felt helpless, staring in anguish at the wounded man,

wanting to help – not knowing what.

'You can do something.'

His voice was faint. She bent over and tears misted her eyes as she looked at the marshal's deathly pale face.

'Get word back to Calvert. My brother is sheriff there. Tell him what happened.'

'Was it them . . . the same as killed Pa?'

'Yeah, Jones and his gang . . . ambushed us . . . Humphrey is sheriff . . . I said that already. Tell him his brother is lying out here . . . tell him . . . tell him to be careful. Tell him I think I recognized Beniah Arnold with Jones.'

Quigley closed his eyes and fell silent.

'I . . . how will I find your brother?'

'If Arnold and Jones join together no place will be safe from them. You make sure you tell Humphrey.'

'I will . . . but I don't know the way.'

Again there was that silence as the dying lawman closed his eyes and was quiet. Then he spoke again.

'Head east . . . you'll come to a big river. Cross over and follow it – you'll come to Calvert.' The eyes were wide open and staring at Gwendolyn. 'You'll do it, kid . . . you got to tell him . . . tell him. . . .' There was a pause and then the lawman spoke again. 'Don't hang about . . . go . . . go now . . . take my badge an' my gun. That way Humphrey will know. . . .'

A long sigh followed. Gwendolyn waited for more. But she waited in vain. Marshal Quigley had spoken his last words and joined his comrades in death.

'I'm sorry, Marshal Quigley.'

She slipped his badge in her pocket, then took his gun from the holster and pushed it inside her waistband. She stood and looked around her at the spread of bodies. She noted Julian Bean who had tended her father's wound. She couldn't remember the other names.

'I reckon a prayer wouldn't come amiss.' Gwendolyn mumbled scraps of Biblical verses remembered from evening prayer sessions with her father. 'Amen,' she finished. 'May your souls rest in peace.'

Trying to avert her eyes from the awful sights around her, Gwendolyn stumbled from the place but did not get far before she bent over again retching violently. There little or nothing to bring up for she had already emptied her stomach, and she had eaten hardly anything over the past few days. There was just a thin substance that left a vile taste in her mouth.

Back at the waterhole she washed her mouth out but it did nothing for the bitter taste. Wearily she hunkered down and stared into the pool seeing her image reflected there. Her face was hollow and pale and her eyes deep pits of despair.

What a sight I am, she thought.

She put her hand up and brushed ineffectively at loose tendrils of hair, then stopped. As she fingered the strands of straw-coloured hair the idea came.

'They thought I was a fella,' she mused thoughtfully, remembering the posse mistaking her for a young man.

Using the knife she hacked at her hair. It was awkward work but she had the pool for her mirror. She ran her fingers through the untidy mop of hair.

'Gwendolyn is dead,' she said to the image in the water. 'I'll guess I need a new moniker. Glen. Howdy, Glen Caruthers. Welcome to hell.'

16

Sheriff Humphrey Quigley stood weighing the badge in his hand. Gwendolyn waited, her hands stuffed deep in her pockets trying to fit into the image she had of the young man, Glen Caruthers.

'Son of a bitch. You say you never saw what happened?'

'No sir, I came across them lying there, all shot up.'

'Son of a bitch. All dead you say, just except Harold? Was he suffering much?'

'I don't reckon so. He just lay there quiet like and talked.'

'I need a drink. I'd be obliged if you'd accompany me down the Twisted Snake.'

Once in the saloon, Sheriff Quigley ordered a whiskey.

'Hell Baron, leave the bottle. I just got some bad news. I need to drown my sorrows.'

'I'm sorry to hear that, Sheriff.' The fat barman put a bottle and a couple of glasses on the bar. 'What sort of bad news?'

'This young fella just told me my brother Harold is dead. Gunned down by Ernest Jones and his gang in an ambush.'

'Goddamnit, Sheriff, that sure is awful. Here.' The barman poured the whiskey. 'Have this on the house. What about your messenger of doom here; what's he drinking? Sure don't look old enough to be drinking nothing but his ma's milk.'

'This kid is tougher than he looks. Rode all the way from Little Buffalo waterhole to bring me the news. Brought me Harold's badge and his gun.' Sheriff Quigley downed his drink in one go and refilled his glass along with one for his young companion. 'Here you are, kid. Drink up.'

The sheriff emptied his glass again. Gwendolyn tossed back the drink just as she had seen the sheriff do. As the raw whiskey hit the back of her throat Gwendolyn felt an excruciating burning sensation cutting a trail all the way down her gullet. It was as if someone had poured molten lava into her.

Gwendolyn gasped and quickly grabbed for the edge of the bar. Raw alcohol poured into a belly that for days had made do with little or no food had a catastrophic effect. A paroxysm of coughing took hold and this, along with a smouldering nausea, left her helpless as she clung to the bar. Her distressed condition was not helped by the sound of raucous laughter from the fat barman.

'Haw, haw, haw, sure a tenderfoot, fool kid you got there, Sheriff.'

That was the last thing she heard before she slid to the sawdust.

When she woke again Gwendolyn lay feeling weak and helpless. Her head ached, her stomach ached and she felt as if she had fallen down the well at home and been dragged back out again.

She opened her eyes and flinched at the brightness of the light. Gradually she was able to focus and realized she was lying on a bunk. It smelt almost as bad as she felt. Then she noticed the bars; horizontal bars that ran from floor to ceiling. She sat up suddenly and immediately regretted her hasty movement. Her head began to spin and she put her hands up and covered her face.

'Oooh . . . I do feel bad!'

Gwendolyn swung her legs off the bunk and sat on the edge holding her head in her hands. Finally she looked around again and it was as she had suspected. She was in jail.

'What did I do?' she whispered as she contemplated the

bars of her cell. 'I can't remember a thing. That whiskey – ugh, I must have done something terrible when I was drunk. But I don't remember nothing.'

A grunting sound somewhere to her right brought her around to stare in apprehension. There was a cell next to hers and a man was moving about in the bunk.

'Son of a bitch!'

Her neighbour sat up and Gwendolyn stared with some uneasiness as she recognized Sheriff Quigley. Like Gwendolyn, he sat on the edge of the bunk and put his head in his hands.

'Son of a bitch,' he said again, then looked across at Gwendolyn. 'I see you're awake, kid.' He gave a wry smile. 'I hope you don't feel as bad as you look.'

With a grunt Sheriff Quigley stood and stretched mightily. The lawman walked across to the cell door, opened it and came out. He walked past Gwendolyn's cell and through another door and disappeared. Gwendolyn stared after him. He stuck his head back around the door.

'Come on then, you like your cell so much you going to take up lodgings in there?'

Gwendolyn put a hand out and tested the cell door. To her relief it opened and she followed the sheriff into his office.

'I . . . I'm not under arrest, am I?'

Sheriff Quigley could not answer for his mouth was wide open in a huge yawn. He gave a snort which might have been a chuckle or a grunt. He looked quizzically at the youngster.

'Why, have you done anything as I need arrest you?'

'No . . . I just. . . .' Gwendolyn shrugged helplessly. 'I woke up in a cell.'

For a moment Sheriff Quigley regarded his young charge. 'You got anywhere to stay, kid?'

'No but . . . I guess I'll find somewhere.'

Sheriff Quigley grabbed up a hat and rammed it on his head then belted a gun rig around his waist.

'Let's go get some breakfast.'

Gwendolyn grabbed up her own hat and followed the sheriff out of the office.

The sign outside the eatery read: Brenda's is Best. Brenda was a youngish woman with red hair tied up in a bun. As soon as she spied the sheriff she came over, her face grave.

'Humphrey, I'm so sorry. I heard the news about Harold.'

'Thanks, Brenda,' the sheriff grunted. 'By the way this is Glen Caruthers. He brought in the news.'

'Welcome, Glen.' Brenda reached out and hugged Gwendolyn. 'Set yourselves down and I'll bring your eats. The usual for you, Humphrey?'

'Nah, just coffee – black and strong.' The sheriff looked suddenly shamefaced. 'Afraid, after news of Harold's death I went down the Twisted Serpent and had myself a bellyful of whiskey. I couldn't eat a thing.' Then he grinned. 'Had to carry this young'un back down the jail. Passed out after one drink. Had to spend the night in the cells.'

'You poor thing.' Brenda reached out and patted Gwendolyn's shoulder. 'Humphrey, I sure hope you ain't going to lead this young fella astray.'

'Yeah, yeah, just get him something to eat.'

Gwendolyn didn't feel hungry but when the plate of bacon and eggs was placed on the table, the smell and the sight of the food worked on her stomach juices loud enough for Sheriff Quigley to hear.

'Damn me, when did you last eat?'

Gwendolyn blushed deeply. For the life of her she couldn't remember when last she had set down to such excellent food.

'Get that inside you.' Brenda looked fondly at Gwendolyn. 'You look as if you were starved of good food for most of your life.'

'Hell, he is a skinny runt. Eat up, kid. We'll need to put some meat on those bones.'

Gwendolyn did clear up everything in front of her, and as she ate Sheriff Quigley sat opposite, drinking coffee and brooding.

'Guess I'll have to organize a burial party to go out and recover those bodies.' The sheriff gazed moodily at Gwendolyn. 'Don't suppose you'd take on the job of leading them back to the place you found them?'

'Me, I. . . .' Gwendolyn shuddered as she remembered the bloody killing field. She looked at the man opposite her – saw the grieving in his face. 'I guess. . . .' she said lamely.

17

The wagons rolled into town drawing curious onlookers into the street to watch. A slim, boyish figure rode at the head of the convoy. Looking neither left nor right Gwendolyn proceeded to the sheriff's office where she pulled up and swung down from the saddle. Sheriff Quigley emerged on to the boardwalk and stared sombrely at the wagons as the drivers hauled up.

'You done it then,' Sheriff Quigley nodded to the youth. 'Good work.'

Gwendolyn nodded in return but said nothing.

'OK, boys, take the wagons down the coroner. I'll round up help for you. You've done enough bringing the bodies this far. I'll get someone to unload for you.' The sheriff turned back to Gwendolyn, 'Glen, you go down Brenda's and get some grub. I'll catch up with you later.'

'Thanks, Sheriff.'

Sheriff Quigley watched the youth walk away then turned to organize the delivery of the bodies recovered from the site of the ambush.

Brenda's eatery was empty, for her customers had all crowded into the street to see the arrival of the wagons and hopefully get a glimpse of their grisly cargo.

'You look done in, child,' Brenda chided. 'Sit down there and I'll fix you a feed. We'll start you off with biscuits and molasses.'

Gwendolyn sank wearily into a seat and felt a surge of gratification as Brenda fussed over her. It was almost as if Brenda was the big sister she never had and Gwendolyn began to relax as she ate. It had been a harrowing few days. Brenda came and sat with her.

'Where are your folks, Glen?'

'Dead.'

'What about brothers or sisters?'

'I was an only child.'

'Ain't you got no one?'

'I reckon not.'

'You poor thing. Where were you heading afore the massacre?'

Gwendolyn shrugged. 'Nowhere.'

The biscuits and molasses tasted wonderful after trail food with a bunch of men who never cooked anything more complicated than beans and coffee. At night when they camped they vied with each other to see who could perform the loudest and longest farts. They had tried unsuccessfully to get Gwendolyn to join in.

'Do you know what you're going to do now?' Brenda pressed.

'I ain't got nothing in mind. I'll just ride, I guess.'

Gwendolyn had not thought further than the completion of her mission. Marshal Harold Quigley had asked her to bring news of the ambush to his brother and that she had done. Then Sheriff Humphrey Quigley had asked her to assist in the recovery of the bodies. Now that was accomplished the realization suddenly hit her that the future stretched emptily before her. The door opened and the sheriff came in. His face was pale and he was breathing heavily.

'Goddamnit!' he said before remembering where he was. 'Begging your pardon, Brenda. I wasn't thinking straight. I had to come away from there. Seeing Harold like that just plumb upset me.'

'Humphrey, sit you down. I'll bring you a mug of coffee. That'll calm you apiece.'

'Nah, Brenda, thanks all the same. I'm heading down the Twisted Serpent. I need something stronger than coffee. Just popped in to see how our young friend is.'

'I'm OK, Sheriff, thank you.'

'Look son, I never really thanked you for what you did for Harold. When you finished here come down the saloon and tell me again about what happened. Would you do that for me?'

Sheriff Quigley looked so forlorn Gwendolyn felt a stab of compassion for him. She had been feeling sorry for herself, not knowing what was going to happen to her and now this man who had suffered as she had suffered was asking for sympathy.

'Yeah, I'll come down,' she said. 'In fact I'll come now.'

When the pair walked into the saloon it was crowded and noisy. There was a momentary silence as the throng noticed the sheriff and his sidekick then the noise struck up again. There was plenty to talk about. Much drink was consumed

70

and a lot of hot air vented as men discussed the massacre of the posse and the death of the sheriff's brother. Centre of attention were the men who had gone out in the wagons to recover the bodies and they were being pumped for gory details of the expedition.

'Whiskey!' Sheriff Quigley grunted to the same fat barman who had served them on their previous visit.

'I see you brought that hard-drinking gent with you tonight, Sheriff. You think a glass of milk might be too strong for him.'

'Baron, for once shut your fool mouth and put up a bottle for me and a sarsaparilla. No, on second thoughts cancel the whiskey. Make that two sarsaparilla.'

Baron took one look at the sheriff's face and moved to quickly fulfil the order.

'Come, Glen. We'll sit somewhere we don't have to look at that fat fool behind the bar.'

There was nowhere to sit in the crowded barroom and Quigley led the way outside. He put his forearms on the hitching rail in front of the saloon and leant on it, staring moodily past the horses tied there. Gwendolyn joined him and together they sipped the sweet drink.

'Sorry about Baron, back there. He's a good man but he's going to rib you each time you come in his saloon. I had to slap him down for your sake.'

'Thank you, Sheriff. Though I guess I did make a fool of myself last time.'

'Aw, you were tired and hungry and not used to drinking. An' that's not a bad thing. Whiskey's been the ruination of many a good man.'

They were silent then, staring out into the night, the noise of the saloon behind them, the quiet of the dusk dropping now upon the town like a gossamer veil, softening the outline of buildings.

71

'We were rivals, Harold and me,' Humphrey Quigley said at last. 'From when we were boys each wanted to beat the other at things – anything – riding, shooting hunting. Even as lawmen we were striving to outdo the other – be the best – collar the most troublemakers.'

Gwendolyn was silent, not knowing how to respond to these confidences.

'Tell me again what happened out at that waterhole.'

So Gwendolyn repeated what she had told him before.

'You say a prayer or words or anything, when Harold passed away?' the sheriff asked when she trailed off her narrative.

'Yes, it wasn't much – some Bible things. I'd never done anything like that afore.'

'You got any brothers, Glen?'

'No, there was just me.'

'Where's your family?'

'I ain't got no one no more.'

'Where are you heading from here?'

Brenda had asked the same question and there was still no obvious answer in Gwendolyn's mind.

'Just riding . . . I guess.'

'I see, drifting. I could do with an assistant, a deputy, if you feel like sticking around. Don't pay much but. . . .'

Sheriff Quigley trailed off, taking a sideways look at the slim figure beside him, thinking maybe he mightn't be up to the job, but then the sheriff owed the youngster a debt.

'Me, I don't know nothing about the law.'

'Hell, nobody does at the start. You learn as you go. What about it?'

Gwendolyn was hesitant, wondering what had prompted the sheriff to make the offer.

'I guess, maybe I will, if you're sure?'

'Sure I'm sure.' Suddenly he was grinning at her. 'Seeing as you got nowhere to stay for now, you can sleep at the jail.'

18

'Goddamnit, Ben, stay on your feet.'

The warning was hissed. There was a strict no-talking rule while working in the quarry. Any infringement and the guards waded in with rifle butts. Ben swayed unsteadily. His injuries sustained during his initiation to the prison still bothered him when out on the chain gang and expected to swing a pick.

All around them men sweated and worked in the baking sun. Some had picks and some had heavy hammers and swung them with varying amounts of enthusiasm or energy depending on what way the guards were looking. Once the rock was pounded to rubble the prisoners filled baskets and carried them to waiting wagons where it was loaded. The wagons belonged to a local freight company and the rock was bought by the railroad.

The toil, as well as being backbreaking, was never ending. Laden wagons trundled from the quarry from early morning till nightfall. The waiting drivers lounged in the seats or stood about talking to the guards.

Ben swayed unsteadily, raised his pick and let it drop on the rock he was working on, the pain from his injured body not allowing him to put much force into the strike. Each time Ben lifted the pick it felt as if a knife was being driven into his chest. He swore and muttered and worked as best he could. At regular intervals the guard who had beat Ben on that first day strolled around to taunt him.

'You don't look too good today. You'll have to do better

than that, you lickspittle.'

Sometimes he hit Ben just for the hell of it. Ben gritted his teeth and stared at the rock and thought he saw the guard's face carved in the surface and drove his pick savagely at the image. But it was only rock and his pick bounced back and Ben felt the sickening wrench of pain as his bruised body protested.

'Keep going, Ben,' Douglas encouraged. 'Soon we'll be drinking rye and chasing the dancing girls.'

'Hell, the only thing I'll chase is my bed. I won't surface for a fortnight.'

'You're young; when a filly fluffs her skirt at you, you'll be raring to go.'

A new group of wagons drew into the loading area. The men driving the teams seemed a different breed from the usual drovers. They were surly, hard-faced men.

A tall, lanky man wandered over to watch the prisoners and stopped near Ben Truman and William Douglas. He idled for a moment while he made himself a quirley. As he worked the tobacco he kept his eyes on William Douglas. The scar-faced convict moved casually nearer the newcomer who turned away and as he did the tobacco pouch fell to the ground.

'Damn my clumsy fingers,' the man muttered and bent over to retrieve his tobacco.

It was done so swiftly only Ben saw Douglas retrieve the gun tucked into the man's belt underneath his jacket. Then Douglas was swinging his pick again and the gun was hidden inside his pants. He winked at Ben and the youngster knew the escape plan, organized via the letters he had written for Douglas to his cousin Ernest, was beginning.

The sudden disturbance startled everyone. A brawl had broken out at the wagons. In direct contravention of orders convicts were moving towards the fight. The guard had come up again to bait Ben. Knowing everyone was looking towards the fight by the wagons he pushed Ben against the rock face and raised the rifle over the youngster.

'Wait. . . .' Ben struggled ineffectually against the brute strength of the guard.

The cruel face was leering at the youth. Suddenly the guard's expression changed. His mouth opened as if he was about to yell but a dirty hand came from behind and closed on his face shutting off his cry.

The guard's eyes bulged with some inner shock. Slowly he sank to the ground and Ben saw the hand clamped on the guard's face belonged to William Douglas. As the guard was lowered to the ground Ben saw the pickaxe jutting from the man's back. Dark ugly blood stained the shirt. Douglas let go his hold and the stricken guard settled lifelessly to the ground.

'Quick,' hissed Douglas, 'take that rifle.'

Ben did as he was told and armed with the rifle waited for the next move from Douglas. The convict was crouched forward with a revolver in his hand. It was as if he were waiting for some signal. Ben waited too, his tension growing. Douglas scanned the rim of the quarry and Ben looked up. There was movement against the skyline and just then armed men appeared along the edge and began firing down into the quarry. Suddenly everything was bedlam.

There was the thunderous roar of rifles as the men on top fired down into the quarry. They were targeting the guards but in the confusion some of the convicts were hit also. Men were yelling and scrambling to get out of the line of fire. Some of the guards tried to return fire but as soon as a rifle was fired it became a target for half a dozen marksmen.

'Come on!' Douglas yelled and plunged forward with Ben following.

A guard loomed up in front of Douglas. He had his rifle

aimed at the fleeing convict. Douglas did not hesitate. He raised his own weapon and pulled the trigger and nothing happened. The guard grinned.

'You're dead, Douglas.'

Behind him Ben witnessed the confrontation. Without thinking – almost without aiming – he fired the rifle he had taken from the dead guard. The shot hit the guard in the shoulder just as his own weapon went off. He staggered back opening his mouth in shock and then went down, dropping his rifle as he fell. Douglas jerked, as the bullet, instead of hitting him dead centre, took him in the side. The convict reeled and clasped his hand to the wound. Ben was immediately alongside his partner. Holding his rifle in one hand he put his other arm around the wounded man.

'Hold on to me,' he yelled.

'Head for the wagons. They'll take us out.'

Ben staggered forward, his companion hanging heavy on his arm. He contemplated throwing away the rifle in order to better help his wounded companion but the thought of a guard confronting them again made him hold on to it.

All around them the noise of gunfire was deafening as the gunmen up above continued shooting into the quarry and guards returned fire. Men were yelling amidst a whirling of action as convicts and guards cowered behind piles of rock or large boulders. Ben's breath was burning in his chest as he staggered forward, his body racked with agony.

'Keep going, you son of a bitch,' he yelled.

The weight of Douglas was dragging more and more and Ben felt his legs weak as he forced himself to keep going. They were nearing the wagons but Ben wondered if they would get there before a guard spotted them. Somehow he managed to keep upright even though his tortured body screamed at him to stop and lie down and die. Then they were through the worst of the chaos and at the wagons.

Convicts had already scrambled aboard. A big, bearded man spotted them.

'Douglas, you son of a bitch.'

Then he was on the other side of the wounded convict and the burden lessened on Ben.

'Make way there,' the bearded saviour yelled. 'Injured man here.'

Helping hands reached out and Douglas was roughly pulled aboard. The bearded man turned to Ben.

'Good work, son. Can you use that rifle?'

'Sure thing,' gasped Ben.

'Start shooting then. The sons of bitches are starting to fight back.'

To emphasize his words bullets thudded into the woodwork of the wagon. A man yelled out as a bullet took him in the throat. Blood gushed out in a fountain and splashed on his companions. The bearded man ran to the front of the wagon and climbed aboard.

'Come on, climb up here and keep me covered.'

Ben clambered up into the passenger seat and turned his rifle towards the guards in the quarry.

'Get up there, you goddamn bitches,' the driver yelled at the horses and the wagon lurched forward.

Ben kept firing, not trying to hit anything but just hoping to keep the guards from accurate shooting. He wasn't sure if he was effective or not. Two more of the convicts in the wagon were hit before the vehicle wheeled out of range. The gunfire faded as the horses picked up speed and headed away from the quarry and the penitentiary.

The breakout had succeeded. It had been messy and brutal and men lay dying or wounded back at the quarry. In the back of the wagon there were more gunshot victims. But the wagon was carrying the occupants to freedom.

19

The Death's Head Saloon in Drygulch Canyon was rowdy most nights but tonight the rafters were ringing with the sound of men celebrating as only fighters can after a victory. Ben Truman, still bemused at the change in his fortunes, sat in the midst of the revelry. The youngster had been welcomed into the Jones' gang as a friend of William Douglas. Ben had discovered William was cousin to the infamous outlaw, Ernest Jones, who had organized the breakout from the penitentiary.

It was a bewildering change of fortune and Ben sat amongst killers and rapists and robbers and drank with them and sang their bawdy songs in the Death's Head Saloon. But then, his spell in Sandell Penitentiary had accustomed him to brutal and violent company.

'To a good man, Ben Truman,' roared Jones raising his glass and grinning at the youngster. 'How would you like to join me in a little enterprise? I thought to take William with me but as he's still laid up you can take his place.'

'Sure, what kind of job?'

Jones roared with laughter then used his finger to tap his head.

'Ernest Jones doesn't reveal nothing till the time is ripe. That's what has kept me ahead of the law. Only I know the nature of the job and the target. That way there can be no leaks and no posse waiting to take me down.'

A few days later Ben rode out with Ernest Jones and his gang, not knowing what it was he was getting into or where they were heading.

Early in the morning after riding all night they came to the outskirts of a town. Ben saw the town sign and wondered what Fullerton held that attracted the attention of Ernest Jones and his gang.

Fullerton was a flourishing community through which the Namath River ran. It was a traditional western town with a wide thoroughfare. Initially the first settlers had built exclusively in timber and the older part of the town was devoted to places of business with false fronts. But as the town grew and prospered the more ambitious citizens began to build in brick and stone, erecting roomy houses and even stores and offices in these more durable materials.

The citizens, on the whole, were respectable law-abiding people who attended the fine brick church and banked their wealth in the imposing two-storey stone building in Seraph Street.

It was early morning and not too many people were stirring as the band of horsemen rode into town and turned into Seraph Street. The riders pulled up and sat their horses.

'Beniah, you keep a watch on the street. Roy and Ben and Carl, you come with me. Time to go get Mr Blatch out of bed. I need the bank open so as to make a withdrawal.'

There were chuckles from the gathered horsemen.

'Sure thing, Ernest, let's go.'

The men peeled away from the main body and rode through the town till they came to an imposing stone-built house. It was surrounded by neat gardens with shady trees. A white painted picket fence enclosed the property. The riders dismounted and tied their horses to the fence before walking up to the front door. With a flick of his head Jones sent Gibbons and another outlaw around the back of the house while he waited at the front with Ben.

'Wakey, wakey,' he said sotto voce and rattled the well-polished knocker.

The door opened and a man in white shirt and grey vest looked out. His tie was draped around his neck as if he had been in the act of tying it in place.

'Yes, what is it?'

'Mr Blatch?'

'Yes, who wants to know?'

When the outlaw chief smiled it held unpleasant undertones.

'My name is Ernest Jones. I want to make a withdrawal from your bank.'

Blatch frowned, then took a watch from his pocket and consulted it.

'Mr Jones, in just over an hour the bank will open for business. If you go down there and wait, I shall arrive shortly and after a consultation with my staff the bank will open its doors. At that point you will be most welcome to conduct your business.'

From somewhere inside came a crash followed by a scream. The bank manager started and looked over his shoulder. While the man was distracted Jones took the opportunity to pull his gun. He shoved the weapon in Blatch's stomach.

'Mister, this is a gun in your belly. The scream you just heard was because my men broke in your house and are holding your wife and daughter.'

'What ... you ... what do you want? Don't hurt my family.'

'Your family will be quite safe as long as you do exactly as I tell you. You will finish dressing and then we will go down to the bank where you will open the safe for me. If you resist or refuse then you and your family will suffer. The men in there with your wife and daughter are rough men. If I tell them to keep your family safe then they will be safe. If I say otherwise those men will do things to your family ...

80

unpleasant things. . . . You understand?'

Blatch opened his mouth, gulped a few times but was unable to speak. Jones rammed the barrel of his gun harder into the soft belly of his victim.

'Understand?' he said harshly.

'Y-yes . . . yes, I'll do as you say.' Blatch was trying to shrink away from the object jammed into his midriff.

'Good. Now finish dressing, kiss your wife and daughter goodbye, and tell them you'll see them later. Tell them to be good and not annoy my men too much.'

Sheriff Tomalley saw the large number of men gathered on Seraph Street and knew immediately what was happening. After all, it was he who had passed on the information regarding the bank and the likely amount of cash held in the big safe. Tomalley was not a vindictive man but Thomas Blatch had turned down the sheriff's request for a loan on account he had not repaid the funds he had previously borrowed.

Sheriff Tomalley ignored the horsemen and padded on down the street heading for his breakfast. On the way he met Thomas Blatch, walking towards the bank. The sheriff ignored the unsavoury looking riders keeping pace with the bank manager.

'Morning, Thomas. You're looking a bit peaky this morning.'

Indeed the bank manager was pale and distraught. He nodded in response to Tomalley's greeting but carried on without speaking. Cheerfully the sheriff kept on walking.

There was a stirring of interest amongst the band of riders as they saw the trio approach. Blatch stopped at the bank, unlocked the front door and stepped inside closely followed by Ernest Jones and Ben.

Ben's unease was growing as they went into the bank. Now the reality of the bank robbery was underway he was filled with apprehension. But it was with a sudden burst of realism he knew he had no other choice. Circumstances had placed him with the gang and he knew he had nowhere else to go.

Once inside, Jones roughly pushed the bank manager towards the offices.

'OK Blatch, now it's time for you to do your stuff and open that safe.'

'I . . . I can't open it yet. It's on a time lock. There's no way of opening it till ten o'clock.'

Jones punched the bank manager full in the face. The stricken man staggered back and went down. The bandit chief towered over him, his gun aimed at the bank manager.

'You stupid son of a bitch,' he yelled. 'Why didn't you tell us that?'

'I . . . I thought you knew,' Blatch stammered.

There was blood on his face and he looked terrified. Jones's hand was shaking as he aimed the gun.

'I ought to plug you right now, you son of a bitch.'

The bank manager moaned and curled into a defensive ball. Angrily, Jones kicked him. At that moment a young man and woman came inside the bank. They stared at the scene before them in alarm – armed men and their boss on the floor.

'What the—'

The youngster's words were cut off as Jones aimed his Colt at him.

'Who the hell are you?' the outlaw chief snarled.

'We . . . we work here.'

Jones strode angrily to the door and yelled to the men outside. 'We're stuck here till the damned safe opens. It's on a time lock. We can't do anything till then. Stay alert.' He whirled back inside. 'Ben, go down the banker's house and tell Roy what's happening.'

Ben left on the run to carry the message. Jones pointed to the young bank teller.

'Fix a sign to say the bank's closed today and hang it on the door.'

'What's going on?'

Jones stalked over to the clerk. 'We're waiting for your boss to open the safe for us. We want to make a withdrawal. Now just do as you're told and put that sign up.'

'Yes, sir.'

The youngster went behind the counter. It might have ended without bloodshed but the young clerk decided to be brave. There was a switch behind the counter that triggered a large bell hung on the front of the building. The youngster looked up at the gunmen holding them hostage and decided to risk it. He flipped the switch and dropped out of sight behind the counter. There was a shotgun stashed there also. It had never been fired during the life of the bank. The clerk, smiling grimly, stood up with the weapon in his hands. Outside the bank the bell jangled noisily.

'Son of a bitch,' Jones said as he shot the young bank teller.

20

Sheriff Quigley came into the jail holding a newspaper. Gwendolyn saw the agitated look on the sheriff's face. He waved the paper at her.

'It's him. It's that goddamn Jones again. Went an' broke a passel of convicts out of Sandell Penitentiary.'

'Jones!' Gwendolyn went cold at the mention of the name.

'He's gone and sprung a bunch of murdering varmints from prison. Here, read for yourself.'

Guards slaughtered in mass breakout from Sandell Penitentiary.

She read how the gang had raided the quarry where the convicts were working. In the ensuing mêlée dozens of convicts had turned on their guards and murdered them before escaping.

'That's terrible,' she said at last looking up at Quigley.

'Jones is building up his gang for something. I'm sure of it. That mean bastard doesn't do anything without a reason.'

'I've just remembered something, Sheriff. Marshal Quigley said to tell you something important. I forgot till now. He said I was to tell you he saw Beniah Arnold with Jones.'

Sheriff Quigley had been striding up and down the office. When Gwendolyn spoke he stopped abruptly, stared at her for seconds then went and sat down at his desk. His face was sombre as he looked intently at his deputy.

'Harold told you that – Beniah Arnold?'

'I'm sorry, Sheriff, I should have told you before but with so much happening I forgot.'

But the sheriff wasn't listening to her. He was staring out into space, his eyes dark and brooding.

'Jones and Arnold. No town or bank will be safe with those two on the loose. No wonder they felt strong enough to attack the prison.' Quigley was shaking his head. 'This is a nightmare come to life. Just think how cocky Jones must be feeling to mount a raid on the penitentiary. That took some planning and daring. I fear there is more to come.'

'What do you mean?'

'I mean it looks like Ernest Jones is gathering an army about him. If he feels brash enough to pull a stunt like that at the prison then there nothing he'll stop at and there's nothing we can do to stop him. If he rides out of Drygulch Canyon with that mob of killers he could raid any town he chooses and loot and rape at will.'

'But surely, the authorities could rustle up a posse and take after him.'

'Yeah, and you saw what happened to Humphrey and his posse.'

Sheriff Quigley fell silent, brooding on the grave implications of the breakout from the penitentiary. Gwendolyn was silent also. There was a growing dread within her at the thought of Jones raiding across the country with no one able to stop him.

'From lightning and tempest, from plague, pestilence, and famine, from battle and murder; and from sudden death, good Lord deliver us,' she intoned, remembering the prayer sometimes used by her father.

'Amen!' Sheriff Quigley said fervently.

They both lapsed back into silence, and contemplated the awful spectre of Ernest Jones and his deadly army pillaging the neighbouring towns with the men responsible for law helpless to stop them. The knock on the door roused them from their reverie.

'Come in,' Quigley called.

A suited man wearing a derby on his head opened the door and stepped inside.

'Howdy,' he greeted. 'My name is Nathaniel Shaler.'

'Howdy, Nathaniel. I'm Sheriff Quigley and this is my deputy Glen Caruthers. What can we do for you?'

Shaler closed the door behind him and flipped out a wallet.

'I'm a Pinkerton agent. I've been sent here to find out what I can about the Jones gang.'

'You sure are welcome, Nathaniel. Take a seat; we were just discussing that very problem.'

Shaler grabbed a chair, flipped it around and sat astraddle with his arms folded across the back.

'The way I see it,' Shaler began without preamble, 'we need inside information. If we could turn one of them there outlaws around he would pass us intelligence on the gang's activities and then we could set up some kind of trap for them.'

'That ain't going to happen,' Sheriff Quigley stated gloomily. 'Jones is such a vicious bastard all his men are frightened of what he would do to them if they betrayed him. Jones has his hideout at a place called Drygulch Canyon. It's a regular hell town. No lawman can go anywhere near it. The hills surrounding it act like a fortress. The whole area is a warren of passes and canyons. It'd take the US Army to undertake a raid on Drygulch Canyon and even that might not be enough.'

'In that case we need to get someone in there, posing as a fugitive. I would volunteer myself only Jones knows my face. I had a run-in with him a while back. Took some lead from him but I survived. That's why I was sent down here. My people think I know more about Jones and how he operates than any of my colleagues. You think of anyone as might go in that nest of rattlers and do some digging?'

'I'm trying to think of someone as wants to commit suicide but for the life of me I can't think of a single one.'

'Yeah, it's as I figured. I guess I'll have to ride out there and nose around. If I could capture one of them galoots then I could stake him out over a slow fire and grill some answers out of him.'

'Hell you would,' Sheriff Quigley said laconically. 'Ain't

that against the law?'

'Law be damned! Jones has robbed and murdered his way across three states, not forgetting shooting yours truly here. So don't tell me about the law. That monster has to be stopped by fair means or foul.'

At that moment there was a knock on the door.

'Come in,' Sherriff Quigley called.

A small boy came in holding a folded paper.

'Mr Hurd sent this. He said it was urgent.'

'Telegraph operator,' Quigley said for the benefit of Shaler as he unfolded and read the message. 'Son of a bitch.' He turned and handed the sheet of paper to the Pinkerton man.

'Bank robbery in progress. Stop. Ernest Jones gang. Stop. Need help urgently. Stop. That's it!' Shaler said excitedly. 'We got him. Where's Fullerton? Can we get there in time?'

'Hell, its forty mile north of here. He'll be long gone afore we get there. Still, we got to make the effort. Glen, go get the horses saddled. I'll round up as many men as are willing to ride.'

It was a good hour before the hastily gathered posse rode out of Calvert. Sheriff Quigley set a hard pace. It was a race against time; one where the sheriff was sure the odds were stacked against them. But they rode just the same; grim men with a mission to save a town from the depredations of a vicious outlaw gang. knowing in their hearts they would be too late.

21

The alarm bell was loud enough to be heard all over town. Roy Gibbons, drinking coffee with Mrs Blatch and her daughter heard it. Gibbons went to the window and stared in the direction of the sound. At that moment there was a pounding on the front door.

'Roy, Roy, it's me, Ben.'

'What the hell's going on?' Gibbons growled as he opened the front door.

'Jones sent me down to tell you the damn safe is on a time lock and we got to wait for it to open. Now that damn bell is going off.'

'That'll rouse the whole goddamn town. Take my place here. I'll go up there and find out what the hell's happening.'

When Roy Gibbons arrived at the bank Jones met him at the door.

'Goddamn mess this is,' Gibbons grumbled. 'Why'd no one know about the time lock?'

'Hell I know. Last thing we expected. We just got to hang on and wait.'

Gibbons noted the scared young woman by the counter.

'Who's that?'

'Bank clerk; her boyfriend set off the alarm. It was the last thing he did.'

Suddenly the alarm ceased. Both men looked towards the counter. Robert Blatch stared back owlishly at them.

'I fixed it.'

'I ought to kill that goddamn bank manager,' Jones raged. He still had his gun in his hand and raised it as if to carry out the threat.

'Cool down, Ernest. We need him to open the safe.'

The mad glare faded from Jones's eyes. 'I reckon you're right. What's happening outside?'

As if in answer there came a flurry of shots.

'Looks like the town's beginning to fight back.'

'Beniah can handle that end of it.'

Out in the street Beniah Arnold grinned happily as he organized the defence of Seraph Street.

'Take cover. Use doorways or alleyways or anywhere. Smash in doors if you have to. Shoot anything that shows.'

In a very short time Seraph Street was sealed off. The citizens of Fullerton waited for guidance from Sheriff Tomalley who was nowhere to be found. The outlaws in the bank cursed their ill-luck and glared malevolently at the frightened bank manager who was wondering if he would survive the day unscathed and prayed silently that his wife and daughter were safe.

Back at the Blatch household Ben felt uncomfortable keeping guard over two helpless females. His companion was a swarthy outlaw named Carl Perkins who had a knife scar running from his scalp to the corner of one eye. Now the restraining influence of Gibbons was out of the way, Perkins was becoming restless and was eying up the two females left in their charge.

'Hell, let's have some fun,' Perkins growled. 'Roy said to keep the females here. He didn't say nothing about not having fun with them.'

Mrs Blatch was a middle-aged woman who looked after her appearance and was still attractive. Her daughter was just a frightened schoolgirl clinging to her mother. Ben looked with consternation at the outlaw.

'What the hell you talking about? We supposed to guard them. Jones gave his word they would be safe if the bank manager did as he was told.'

'You dumb kid. You think Jones meant any of that shit? As soon as he has the money from the safe he'll as like as not put a bullet in that goddamn sumbitch.'

'It ain't right, I tell you.' Ben was shaking his head. 'I ain't having none of it.'

Suddenly Perkins turned his gun on Ben.

'You do as you're told, you sumbitch. I'm in charge here. You're just a wet-nosed kid. Hell, I don't suppose you ever had a proper woman afore. Just you do as you're told.'

'No!' Ben yelled. 'I ain't going to let you harm them women.'

With a swift movement the gun slammed into the side of Ben's face. He staggered back, blood pouring down his cheek.

'Damn you!'

Perkins was pointing the gun at Ben.

'I ought to shoot you, you goddamn bastard kid. In fact I might just do that.'

Ben wondered if he could dive beneath the gun and tackle the outlaw. There was a flurry of movement as the women cowered back from the action. Perkins swung round and fired over their heads, taking out a window.

'Stay still, you sumbitch!' he screamed.

Ben took his chance and launched himself at the man, and as he crashed into him they fell across the kitchen table. Ben grabbed for and got a grip on the hand that held the gun.

'Goddamn, I'm going to kill you sumbitch!'

With his free hand Ben punched as hard as he could against the side of the gunman's head. The man's knee came up into Ben's groin sending agonizing pain through him.

'Aaaagh!'

In spite of the agony Ben held on to the gun, for he knew, given the chance, Perkins would kill him. He had a slight advantage for he was sideways on to the gunman, who could not bring his other hand into the fight. Again he punched, hitting the gunman on the point of the jaw.

'Damn!'

The gun went off but Ben didn't see where the bullet went. Ben had been in a few saloon brawls in the past and knew it was imperative to disable his adversary as quickly as possible, so he punched again into the face of his opponent.

Perkins was yelling incoherently as he struggled. He tried to bring the gun to bear on Ben but the youngster held his own, keeping the weapon pointed harmlessly away from him. All the time he kept punching and this was beginning to have an effect.

Perkins tried to pull himself off the table, but Ben strenuously resisted. His fist was sore and bloody but he couldn't stop till he had his opponent helpless. Perkins suddenly let go the gun and snapped Ben's grip on his wrist. With a quick movement he gripped Ben by the neck, fingers like wire grips clamping on the youngster's throat.

Ben tried to pull away, lost his footing and went down with the outlaw on top. He hit his head on the stone floor and for a moment saw stars. The fall did not break the choke grip on his neck.

'You sumbitch,' Perkins yelled, 'I'm going to kill you.'

Ben could not reply for the hold on his neck was tightening and cutting off his wind. Desperately he grabbed at the hands choking him and pulled. There was no movement; it was as if the hands were welded to his neck. He tried punching again. But his opponent buried his face in Ben's chest and the punches bounced harmlessly of the back of the outlaw's head. A red mist was forming across Ben's vision and his lungs were burning as his oxygen was cut off.

'Die, you sumbitch.'

And Ben believed death was creeping over him as he grew weaker and weaker, locked in a brutal grip he was unable to break.

There was a sudden jolt as his assailant flinched under some unseen shock. The grip on Ben's neck slackened. It was enough for him to suck in life-giving air. He looked up and saw someone looming above him. Mrs Blatch was raising some sort of club over her head. Ben watched as she brought it down for the second time on the head of the man holding him down. There was a solid chunk and Perkins sagged to the floor.

Ben sucked in precious air while massaging his throat and stared up at Mrs Blatch. Her eyes were wild and she was clutching a rolling pin in both hands. For a moment Ben thought she was about to clout him with her improvised weapon.

'Thank you, ma'am,' he wheezed, massaging his throat, 'you sure saved my bacon.'

'You going to hurt us, young man?'

'Ma'am, I ain't in any fit state to hurt anyone. And I don't make war on women. Leastways not one as can handle a rolling pin like you.'

Mrs Blatch lowered her improvised club.

'I guess you tried to save us from that filthy beast. I thank you for that. How are you? You look a bit shaky.'

Ben climbed unsteadily to his feet.

'I must admit, I've had better days. My throat feels like I been swallowing gravel.'

'What about him?' Mrs Blatch pointed her rolling pin at the outlaw sprawled on the floor beside Ben. 'When he comes to he'll start making trouble again.'

'If you got any rope I'll tie him up.'

'You're a good man, mister. Why are you riding with this trash? You don't belong with them no more than my Blatch does. Oh, dear God, I wonder how he is. Did you see him?'

'Yes, ma'am, I seen him up at the bank afore I come down here. He was fine.'

Just then a burst of gunshots could be heard from the direction of the town. Ben cocked his head, listening.

'Seems to me Jones has run into some trouble,' he said. 'Maybe I ought to get back up there.'

He turned to go but felt a hand on his arm restraining him.

'Don't go, son. Like I said you don't belong with them.'

For long moments Ben stared into Mrs Blatch's eyes.

'I . . . I wish that were true, but I don't belong nowhere else.'

22

Ten o'clock came and the time lock released its grip on the safe.

'Get that goddamned safe opened,' Jones snarled at Blatch.

The bank manager was dishevelled and haggard, his face dirtied with blood. Wearily he did as he was told.

Out in the street the outlaw gang was coming under fire as some of the braver citizens tried sniping at Jones's men. Two of the outlaws had taken bullets and Beniah Arnold was becoming angry.

'Right, you sons of bitches,' growled Arnold. 'Let's teach

those goddamn townsfolk a lesson.' He pointed across the street at the hardware store. 'Get some kerosene and set this goddamn town on fire. That'll smoke the bastards out in the open and then we can kill a few.'

It was quickly done and soon flames licked hungrily at dry timber buildings and then roared into conflagration. Smoke billowed out across the street and under cover of this Arnold led a group of outlaws towards the place he had noted the shooting was coming from. The marksmen were caught unawares as they stood up from their cover the better to see what was happening down in the street. Arnold did not have to direct his men in the attack; they were all seasoned gunmen. Shots rang out with devastating effect and men fell under the firepower of the outlaw gang.

'Get some more of those buildings on fire,' Arnold directed. 'Burn everything that'll burn. Some of you watch out for those goddamn townsfolk.'

With whoops of delight the outlaws set to work. Building after building was set alight. Inside the bank, Jones was helping his men empty the safe. They filled saddle-bag after saddle-bag and passed them out the front where they were loaded on the horses.

'Right, Blatch, get inside that safe.'

'But . . . but . . . what about my wife and daughter?'

Jones fired a shot over the terrified man's head. 'Get in the goddamned safe!' he roared and the bank manager did as he was told. Jones slammed the door shut.

'What about the woman?' Roy Gibbons asked, pointing to the terrified clerk.

'Bring her along. We'll use her as a hostage.'

They ran into the street that was looking like a scene from hell. The fires had taken hold and were burning fiercely. Smoke billowed freely and hung over the town in a dark pall.

'Beniah,' Jones roared. 'Time to go.'

Arnold strode out of the smoke, soot-begrimed and with a fierce grin on his face.

'Hell, I ain't had so much fun in a while. You got the loot?'

Jones pointed to the bulging saddle-bags. 'We got loot aplenty.'

'Yippee,' Beniah yelled.

The call was taken up by the outlaws as they mounted up and raced through the town in the direction of the Blatch household. It was time to pick up the men left on guard at the bank manager's home. As they rode they fired off pistols and rifles aiming at buildings and sometimes scoring a hit on windows.

Mrs Blatch had moved into the front parlour with her daughter so they would not have to listen to the ranting of the outlaw tied up on the floor of the kitchen mouthing vile threats. Ben heard the thunder of hoofs and peered through the curtains.

'It's Jones – the whole gang. They must have done the job.'

The horses pulled up outside the house.

'Perkins, Truman, come on. We're hightailing it out of here.'

Ben stared in consternation at the mob of men outside. If they came inside and found Perkins they might want to take revenge on the women. He couldn't let that happen. For a wild moment he contemplated holding them off with his gun but knew his efforts were doomed to failure. Jones could pour so much lead inside the house the womenfolk would be in danger.

'Quick,' he hissed, 'get out the back and hide. Don't come back till you hear us leave.'

'What are you going to do?'

'Just go!' he tried to put a snarl in his voice but failed miserably.

Mrs Blatch reached out and touched Ben's cheek. 'Be safe.'

'I'm coming out,' Ben yelled, and went to the front door. 'Where's Perkins?'

'Some men broke in. Took us by surprise. Killed Perkins and knocked me out cold. What's happening?'

Ben looked dishevelled enough for his story to be believed.

'Hell you say. We ought to go back in that town and shoot a few more.'

'We ain't got time now. Besides we done enough damage as it is. Goddamn half the town is on fire.'

For the first time Ben noticed the smoke. Black clouds swelled over the centre of the town.

'Come on, Truman. We brought your horse. Time to go.'

23

Exhausted and despondent, Sheriff Quigley listened to Sheriff Tomalley while he related the events of the day. When they arrived in Fullerton, the town was well ablaze and Quigley had to decide whether to stay and fight the fire or take off in pursuit of the outlaw gang that had created so much mayhem. In the end he opted for the first choice and his men joined the people of Fullerton in fighting the fires raging through the town.

When the posse arrived, the townsfolk were in a state of panic with Sheriff Tomalley ostensibly unable to take control of the situation. Quigley had to take over and direct the efforts to save the town. While he was thus engaged Mrs Blatch arrived on the scene demanding to know what had happened to her husband. It was only then they learned the bank manager was locked in the safe. Luckily Shaler was equal to the task and was able to communicate with Blatch and ascertain the combination of the safe. They were just in time, for the air inside the safe was running low. It was a joyful reunion for the couple.

Once the fire was under control Detective Shaler began the task of interviewing everyone regarding the day's events and asked Gwendolyn to accompany him. Eventually they came back inside the jailhouse to join Quigley and Tomalley.

'We got a prisoner,' he declared. 'Carl Perkins and another fella were guarding the Blatch family to ensure the bank manager played along and opened the safe for the outlaws. Perkins wanted to abuse Mrs Blatch and her daughter but this other fella tried to stop him and they fought. Mrs Blatch laid Perkins out with a rolling pin.' He grinned suddenly. 'Maybe had some practice on her old man. Mrs Blatch reckons this young outlaw saved their lives as well as their honour.' He turned to Tomalley. 'You got any idea who he was?'

'Nah, I never saw anyone.'

'Another thing, they took a hostage.'

'What the hell . . . a hostage?'

'Yeah, young woman as worked in the bank. Alice Salinger.'

'Pore gal, I don't reckon much to her chances in the clutches of that gang of hellions.'

'What a goddamn blistering mess this is. It gets worse and worse. Jones rides in, bold as brass, robs the bank, kills a passel of folk, sets fire to the town and kidnaps a female clerk. Somehow or other that murdering gang has got to be stopped.'

'My blood runs cold to think what might happen to that hostage. She'll more than likely not survive and if she does she'll maybe wish she hadn't.'

Gwendolyn's insides churned as she listened to Shaler's words, remembering her own ordeal at the hands of the outlaw gang.

'We need inside information. This job would have taken weeks if not months of planning. They would have ridden in here, done a little digging, found out where Blatch lived. Then planned the raid and ridden in with enough men to keep the townsfolk at bay. Blatch says as there was over half a million in that safe. Having done it once Jones will try again. We have to know where.'

'It's like watching out for a prairie fire. You never know where or when it's going to strike.'

'Yeah, and even when you do spot it you can't guarantee you'll be able to handle it.'

Suddenly the door to the jailhouse was thrust open and a distraught woman burst in on the lawmen.

'My Alice, tell me what has happened? Is it true? Has she been taken? Tell me, Sheriff. Tell me it ain't true.'

Sheriff Tomalley lumbered to his feet. 'Mrs Salinger. I'm right sorry. We ain't sure what has happened.'

Gwendolyn watched the woman as she stared wild-eyed at the sheriff. Her fist went to her mouth and Gwendolyn could see her biting her knuckles.

'Sheriff Tomalley, tell me it ain't true. My Alice, she's only eighteen. She was so proud to be working in the bank. Tell me, Sheriff. Tell me the truth.'

'You go on home now, ma'am.' Sheriff Tomalley was ushering the distraught woman towards the door. 'We're still finding out who's missing. I'll let you know as soon as I know anything.'

The scream when it came shocked everyone in the room.

It was the anguished cry of a distraught mother.

'They've taken her. Why don't you tell me?'

Mrs Salinger's face was suffused with an angry red tinge; her eyes were wide and staring. She began to beat on Sheriff Tomalley's chest with clenched fists.

'Tell me! Tell me! Tell me!' She sank to her knees sobbing. 'My Alice, my precious Alice.'

Gwendolyn jumped to her feet and came over to the weeping woman.

'Mrs Salinger.' Gwendolyn was reaching out to the woman. 'We do believe Alice has been taken hostage. They'll probably release her as soon as they think they're safe.'

Eyes, swimming in tears Mrs Salinger looked up at Gwendolyn. 'You think so?'

'We'll do everything we can to get her back.'

The emotions that had kept the woman going seemed to drain away, leaving a bewildered look in her eyes. As Gwendolyn helped her to her feet Mrs Salinger noticed the badge on her vest. She gripped Gwendolyn by the arms staring at her with wide anguished eyes.

'Promise me you'll get her back for me. She's all I have in the world. My life will end if anything happens to my Alice. Promise me.'

Gwendolyn nodded, smiling reassuringly at the woman. 'We'll get her back.'

'Promise me.' Hope was being reborn. 'Promise me. Promise me now.' The words were urgent, the eyes pleading and grief-stricken, the hands gripping forcefully on Gwendolyn's arms. 'Promise me.'

They stood like that, Mrs Salinger looking to Gwendolyn for some sort of reassurance; Gwendolyn feeling the depth of the woman's grief. And the words came out of her mouth unbidden as if it were not Gwendolyn speaking but her assumed character Glen Caruthers uttering the words.

'I promise.'

The woman's arms went around Gwendolyn's neck. 'Bless you, boy, bless you. I do believe you.' There was a new light in Mrs Salinger's eyes as she stood back and regarded the young man before her. 'What's your name? I must know your name.'

'Glen, ma'am.'

'God go with you, Glen. You will save my Alice. I feel it in my heart.'

24

'Son of a bitch, you ain't going nowhere. You work for me and I'm saying no. No! No! No! Is that plain enough for you?'

Gwendolyn stared steadily back at Sheriff Quigley. His face was red and angry.

'I have to do this. You heard me promise Mrs Salinger I would try and get her daughter back.'

Sheriff Quigley's face got redder if that was possible. In the short time he had employed his young deputy he had grown overly fond of him. At times he felt he had lost a brother when Harold was killed but in exchange he had gained a son. He was loath to risk the youngster's life in the mad venture he was embarking upon.

'For gawd's sake, you're only a kid not yet dry behind the ears. I ain't going to have your death on my conscience.' In exasperation Quigley turned to the Pinkerton detective for help. 'What do you think, Nathaniel?'

'Hell, Sheriff, the boy thinks he can do it. Maybe he can pull it off.'

'Goddamn you for a conniving snake in the grass!' Sheriff Quigley roared. 'I thought you'd back me up, not encourage the young whippersnapper. You're a cold calculating son of a bitch. You'd risk this youngster's life to further your own goddamn ambitions.'

Pinkerton detective and sheriff glared at each other.

'If another man without a badge said what you just said to me, we'd be out in that street clawing iron.'

'For two pins I'd take you on anyway.'

Gwendolyn stepped between the two men glowering at each other and looking as if they would come to blows.

'How's that going to help if you two get fighting each other? I'll need some help to pull this off.'

Sheriff Quigley's shoulders slumped. 'Hell, Glen, it was as if Harold had sent you to me to take care of an' here you are proposing to go into that rattlers' nest. I—'

He turned away, his voice gruff and emotional. Gwendolyn realized the man was genuinely afraid for her.

'I'll be careful.'

The sheriff pulled a kerchief from his pocket and blew his nose loudly.

'Hell, if you're hell-bent on getting yourself killed we'd better give you a hand. We need some sort of plan.'

'I've been thinking on this,' Shaler said. 'We got to lead Jones into an ambush. The trap has to be baited.'

Both Sheriff Quigley and Gwendolyn turned to the Pinkerton man.

'We got one of Jones men in jail – Carl Perkins.'

'Yeah, so what?'

'We arrest Glen here an' put him in with Perkins. They make a break for it and Perkins takes Glen back to Drygulch Canyon.'

'Then what?'

'Glen tells Jones he's overheard us discussing plans to bring money into the bank to replace the stolen cash. The pull will be too much and more than likely Jones will come back to repeat his raid.'

'Jones has just robbed Fullerton. He ain't likely to strike twice at the same place.'

'That's right! An' because it ain't likely then it might just tempt him. Lightning doesn't strike twice in the same place. Jones will figure no one will be expecting him to attempt another raid on the Fullerton bank and so soon after the original robbery.'

'What do you think, Glen?'

Gwendolyn shrugged nonchalantly. 'I reckon.'

But already she was regretting the promise made to Mrs Salinger that she would get her daughter back. The pledge was rash and Gwendolyn had made it in the emotional rawness of the moment. For a while she believed she could do it but now the plans were being made regarding the enterprise and she was beginning to feel scared.

Sheriff Quigley was right. She was just a raw kid and here she was preparing to ride into the hideout of the most notorious outlaw the West had ever bred, hoping to lure him back to Fullerton. But now it seemed like it was too late to change her mind, for the two lawmen lost no time in putting the plan into action.

With a lot of shouting and shoving Gwendolyn was brought into Fullerton jailhouse.

'This'll put paid to your thieving,' Sheriff Quigley snarled as he hustled Gwendolyn towards the cells. 'You'll be an old man afore you smell free air again.'

'I never did nothing,' Gwendolyn protested. 'You belly scratchers are making a mistake. I ain't no thief. I was brought up a good, church-going Christian.'

The cell door slammed behind her and Gwendolyn's shoulders slumped. She kicked despondently at the cell door. At last she turned to survey her confinement and noticed Perkins in the next cell.

'Howdy,' offered Gwendolyn. Perkins glowered back at her. 'Hey, you the fella as were in that bank robbery? I heard tell they caught someone. That was some sweet job. I wish I could've been in on it. Cleared the bank out. I heard them talking about bringing in a load of cash to replace the stuff that was stolen.'

Perkins' scarred face, made worse by his fight with Ben Truman, puckered as he peered at the youngster.

'What're you talking about?'

'What happened to your face? You look like you been in a scrap with a cactus at some time and lost out.'

Perkins was suddenly at the bars separating the two cells, gripping them tightly.

'Shut the goddamned hell up about my face. It's my business what happened. Now what the hell you saying about bringing in that cash?'

Gwendolyn stepped back from the bars when Perkins lunged.

'Sorry, friend, I didn't mean no offence. Just a mite curious, that's all.'

'Yeah, well you know that's what killed the cat. Tell me about the cash you said they were bringing in.'

Gwendolyn looked around the cell as if to make sure no one was listening.

'I overheard the lawmen talking with the bank manager fella,' she said in a lowered voice. 'He wanted to know if they were staying around to protect the cash the bank was bringing in to make up for the money lost in the robbery.'

'They're bringing in more money?'

'And then they said they wouldn't be needed when the cash was delivered. They told that bank manager not to worry, for no one was going to attack the shipment as no one knows about it and it weren't likely Jones would attempt to rob the same place twice.'

'Dogdang their mangy hides. I reckon Ernest Jones would give a lot to know about that there bank money.' Now it was Perkins' turn to kick the cell bars. 'An' I'm stuck in here. If I could get word to Jones he'd more than likely storm in here, take that money and spring me out of here.'

'You mean Jones would dare to come back to Fullerton after robbing the bank? After killing all those people and torching the place?'

'You don't know Jones like I do.'

'This Jones, does he take on new people – like if a fella wanted to join him?'

'Yeah sure, there are fellas on the lam from the law and they run to Drygulch Canyon. They can join up with Jones if they choose. Most do. He can rustle up forty, fifty men for a raid if he needs.'

'What if we both bust out of here? Would Jones take me in his gang?'

'What the hell you talking about? We're locked in here tight as horseshoes on a hoof. Now if I had me a gun—'

Gwendolyn stood up, walked over to the cell door and peered towards the outer office. Then, still glancing over her shoulder, she came furtively towards the bars that separated the two cells. She held out her hand; nestling in the palm was a large iron key.

'Sumbitch,' Perkins hissed. 'Where'd you get that?'

'It's what I do – steal things.'

They waited till nightfall. There was no night guard and the escapees crept from the cells. Perkins wanted to arm himself but the gun case was securely locked so they had to do without weapons. They found a row of saddled horses outside the Golden Deuce Saloon and stealing two, rode out of town undetected.

25

Ben Truman was sitting in on a game of poker in the Death's Head Saloon. William Douglas was at the table having recovered from his wound. Drygulch Canyon had its own doctor, a medical man wanted in several states for helping elderly patients to their grave and then helping himself to their wealth. Ben took no notice as someone came in the swing doors. That is, he took no notice till a voice behind him spoke.

'Truman, you dirty double-crosser, I'm calling you out.'

Startled, Ben swung round. Carl Perkins stood, feet braced, with a Colt held steady in one hand.

'Carl, am I glad to see you. I . . . I thought you were dead. Last time I seen you, you were stretched out in that kitchen with a busted head.'

'Stand up, you cussed sumbitch, else I'll shoot you where you sit.'

Ben pushed back his chair and stood.

'Hell, Carl, I ain't got no quarrel with you.'

'You sure as hell have. I got bumps on my head big as goose eggs and a spell in the hooky through you. Now I want reparation. I'm going to kill you. Shoot you down like the miserable dog you are.'

'I swear to God, Carl, I never meant that to happen. I was

only obeying orders. Roy told me to keep the females safe and that was what I was doing. I didn't want us both getting in trouble if something happened to them.'

Unnoticed by either man, Ernest Jones had stepped inside the saloon. He was accompanied by a slim, good-looking youth.

'That's right, Carl, I did give orders to keep them safe.'

Perkins turned towards the voice and that's when Ben moved. He swung his chair and smashed it into Perkins' gun hand. The gun went off, the bullet going somewhere into the saloon. Ben, using the chair like a battering ram, pushed forward. Perkins, cussing vehemently, went backwards as he tried to get the gun lined up on Ben. But Ben was relentlessly thrusting hard with his chair, keeping the gunman off balance so he was forced to back peddle. Perkins snagged his heel, stumbled and went down.

Ben threw himself across the chair, his weight effectively pinning the gunman to the floor. Then he was on him like a wild man, punching hard and fast at the scarred face. Ben was yelling incoherently as he fought. It was almost a repeat of the scene back in Fullerton in the kitchen of the Blatch family home.

Trapped beneath the chair Perkins made the mistake of trying to bring his gun to bear. It was easy for Ben to reach down and trap the gunman's wrist against the floor with one hand while he punched with his free hand.

'Son of a bitch,' Ben yelled. 'You're an ugly cuss and when I'm finished with you, you'll look so goddamned awful your own ma won't recognize you.'

As he yelled, Ben was punching hard and fast. Pinned by the chair, Perkins writhed on the floor unable to counter the attack. Under the onslaught his nose was flattened into a bloody pulp. Blood ran down the his cheeks and dripped into the sawdust. Ben's fist was bloody also but he was relentless in his punishment. He heard someone yelling but took no notice till hands grabbed him and jerked him away from the chair he was using to trap his opponent.

'Enough!'

Even as Ben struggled against the men restraining him a hand reached down and took the gun from Perkins. The gunman made no resistance. In fact he was barely conscious. Ernest Jones came forward and stood looking down at the bloodied man on the floor.

'I do believe you've spoiled his natural good looks, Ben Truman. A couple of you fellas take him across to the saw-bones.' As the men moved to obey him Jones came and stood in front of Ben. 'What really happened between you two?'

Ben sagged in the grip of the men holding him as the steam went out of him now that the danger was over.

'Aw hell, he was fixing to mess with them there females you asked us to keep safe. One of them was only a child. I tried to stop him and he went crazy an' attacked me. I had to lay him out.'

'You told me a lie. You said it was two men came in and attacked you. Why'd you tell that?'

'I . . . I had the idea I'd killed Perkins an' I didn't want to be blamed for his death. I thought you'd be mad at me, so I cooked up that tale about being attacked.' Ben felt a chill up his spine as a pair of cold eyes stared at him.

'I don't like being lied to. For such a crime I've a mind to take you out and have you killed. But I owe you for taking care of my cousin, William. Helped him break out of jail and then saved his life. I'm beholden to you for that, but one more slip and you'll end up in an unmarked grave out in the canyon. Understand?'

'Sure thing, Ernest. I ain't wanting to cross you. I was just looking after your interests. I though you might want those females for hostage if anything went wrong at the bank.'

Abruptly, Jones swung away. 'William, I need you to hear this. I got a fella here as has some interesting news for us.'

William Douglas stood up from the poker game and came over. He slapped Ben on the shoulder as he passed.

'That was a fine bit of action, Ben. But if I were you I'd watch my back. Perkins won't let this go. He's one mean son of a bitch. Pity you didn't kill him when you had the chance.'

Jones and Douglas moved out of earshot and, thinking on what Douglas had said, Ben went back to the poker game. He didn't notice the youngster with Jones watching him covertly.

Gwendolyn was interested in Ben once she cottoned on who he was. It was Ben who had saved the Blatch females from being molested and Gwendolyn realized now that he had done it at great risk to himself. Then she had to give all her attention to Jones as he introduced her to Douglas.

'William, this is Glen Caruthers. He busted out of Fullerton jail with Perkins in tow.'

Douglas eyed the youngster. 'Hell, he's only a kid. What the hell were you in jail for?'

'It was a frame-up. They reckoned I broke in a store and stole some goods. I swear it wasn't me as done it. Fella comes up and offers me this cheap stuff and like a fool I take it not knowing it was stolen and when I tries to sell I'm tagged for the robbery.'

Douglas burst out laughing. 'You'll do, kid. I never knowed a thief yet as owned up to it.'

Jones was grinning also. 'Perkins says as how Glen here, even though he ain't no thief, somehow managed to lift the key from the sheriff so he can unlock the door and walk to freedom.'

Both men were chuckling as they regarded the new recruit.

'What's this interesting news you spoke about, Ernest?'

'Tell him, kid. Tell William here what you told me.'

So Gwendolyn repeated the tale she had related to Perkins while in jail with him.

'Son of a bitch,' Douglas said and looked across at his cousin. 'They're bringing in all that money. I hope you're not thinking what I think you're thinking.'

'Jeez, William, if this is true, it's a gift.'

'You can't do it, cousin – it's too risky. After that raid on the town they'll be all fired up and guarding that money tighter than a steer watching over her calf.'

'That's where you're wrong, cousin. They won't be expecting no raid. What madman would ride into a town he's just raided? In fact, Glen here is telling me that's what he overheard. Them lawmen figured there was no need for much security as they didn't think we would want to go back to raid an empty bank. Ain't that right, Glen?'

26

Sheriff Tomalley was a mite curious about the breakout from his jail. Someone had been able to unlock the cell doors and walk out. The more he thought about it the more curious he became. Two horses had been stolen after the jailbreak but Tomalley knew there was only one prisoner in the cells and that was the bank robber caught at Blatch's house.

As well as his misgivings about the jailbreak, he was concerned by the arrival of numerous strangers in town. Solid looking men, respectably dressed, booking into boarding houses and hotels. Others were workmen arriving ostensibly to help rebuild the burned out buildings that had been torched by the Jones gang. So many outsiders had drifted into the town there wasn't a spare bed to be rented in Fullerton.

Sheriff Tomalley had tried quizzing a few of them. They courteously answered his inquiries giving various reasons for their presence in town. Some claimed to be drummers, others lawyers in town to assess insurance claims on damaged property. Still others alleged they were travelling through and would be continuing on their way after a short stopover. It was all very mystifying and Sheriff Tomalley was troubled by this sudden influx. The more he thought about these matters the more suspicious he became. He would have been more concerned if he knew the newcomers all reported to Shaler after arriving in town, for the Pinkerton detective was calling in reinforcements for the expected strike against the outlaw gang.

'Something's brewing,' he mused. 'And I reckon those lawmen are involved. Why ain't they gone back to Calvert again?'

Casually he broached the subject of the jailbreak to Sheriff Quigley.

'You may remember we brought a young fella with us from Calvert,' Quigley told him. 'I hired him as deputy. Then Shaler caught him looting in a store that was part burned. We locked him in your jail for safekeeping. Now he's gone, along with Perkins. We should have kept a closer watch on him.'

Tomalley pondered on Sheriff Quigley's explanation. He remembered the youngster riding in with Quigley and Shaler. Now Quigley wanted him to believe he was a looter. Tomalley clearly recalled the youngster helping the lawmen. He had also accompanied Shaler when the Pinkerton man set out to find out what he could about the bank robbery.

It all makes sense, thought Tomalley. Quigley is hot for revenge for the killing of his brother. He cooks up this scheme to get someone into Drygulch Canyon. They shove that fella in with Perkins and they both escape. Perkins high-tails it back to Drygulch Canyon with that young fella tagging along. He gets inside Jones' gang. Clever, very clever, Sheriff Quigley. Ernest Jones ought to be warned he has a traitor in his midst.

Sheriff Tomalley had his own system for getting messages to Jones. Drifters coming into town at regular intervals would contact him and the sheriff would give them a message for the bandit chief. He never wrote anything down in case it fell into the wrong hands. His messages were sent verbally and kept simple.

'You have a spy in your camp,' he told the courier.

When the message arrived back at Drygulch Canyon, Ernest Jones called a meeting with Beniah Arnold and his cousin, William Douglas.

'Got word we have an undercover agent inside Drygulch,' Jones informed the two men. He waited for their reaction.

'You got any idea who it is?' said William.

'I have my suspicions but for the present I'm keeping them to myself. I want you to figure it out – see if we come up with the same fella.'

'Hell I know,' Beniah growled. 'I can vouch for my men. I know most of them from way back. Got to be someone in your crew.'

'William?'

'It has to be someone has arrived fairly recent. Sooner we smoke this traitor out the better.'

'That's my thinking too. William, go fetch that friend of yours, Ben Truman.'

Douglas stared hard at his cousin. 'Why for, Ernest?'

'Think about it, William. I've been working it all out since the tip-off came in. You're locked up in Sandell Penitentiary and this young fella makes friends with you. You're my cousin. He helps you escape. What better way to worm his way into my confidence?'

'Ernest, that's bullshit. You think they would go to that sort of bother? It doesn't add up. Hell, Ernest, he saved my life.'

'If he breaks out with you he knows you'll bring him here and vouch for him. Don't you see? He needs you alive to get in.'

'I don't know. Hell, I just don't know—'

'William, I've stayed out of the clutches of the law all this time because I'm a careful man. I'm also a suspicious man. If I suspect someone not being straight with me I just kill him to be on the safe side. Perkins and he were supposed to look after the banker's women. Truman slugs Carl and leaves him to be taken by the law. He makes up a yarn about someone attacking them and killing Perkins. One lie after another.'

When Jones stopped talking the silence in the room stretched.

'Jeez, Ernest, when you put it like that it does sound bad. Maybe you're right and Ben is a lawman.'

'Go fetch him, William.'

With a sigh, Douglas stood up and left the room. When the door closed behind him Jones turned to Arnold.

'Go see if Perkins is recovered enough to sit in on this. After what Truman did to him he'll enjoy beating the information out of him.'

27

Gwendolyn wandered down the livery and found a crusty old-timer in charge.

'I need a place to sleep and a job,' she told him.

'Never knowed anyone round here as would do any work. An' anyways you look too puny.'

'I was raised on a farm. Worked all my life.'

For a moment the liveryman eyed her up. 'Carrying pails of water, fetching bales of hay, cleaning up horse shit.'

'I can do it.'

'Start right away filling up the water trough and when that's done clean out the stalls. I'll see how you shape up.'

It had been a while since Gwendolyn had done any physical labour and as she worked she was poignantly reminded of her days back on the farm. For a moment tears started but she quickly scrubbed her shirt sleeve across her eyes. Fiercely she attacked the jobs she had been set – cleaning and fetching and carrying – and gradually had the livery in tidy order. It felt good to be doing something physical. When she finished she got a broom and began sweeping the yard.

Ted Worth, the liveryman, had taken the opportunity to nip up to the Death's Head Saloon for a beer. When he came back he stood looking round at the orderliness of his stables.

'Dang me, where's that kid got to?'

Hearing noises out back he discovered his new groom sweeping the yard and stood watching. Gwendolyn wiped a shirt sleeve across her sweating face and leaned on the broom.

'Harrumph. Is that how you do your work? I leave you on your own and all you do is use that there broom as a prop.'

Gwendolyn started guiltily. 'I . . . aw . . . I was busy. I did all those jobs you wanted doing. I thought I'd sweep the yard. It looked like it needed sweeping.'

'Mmm . . . I guess you can stay the night. See how you fit in. Don't like slackers. What's your name?'

'Gwendol . . . Glen . . . Glen Caruthers.'

'OK, Glen. You pick yourself a place to sleep. No smoking, mind you.'

'Gee, thanks, mister. I don't smoke.'

'An' no bringing no females back here, mind.'

'No sir, no females. I just need a place to sleep.'

As she snuggled down into the comfort of her improvised bed up in the hayloft, Gwendolyn couldn't stop yawning, and though she wanted to think over recent events and develop a plan of action, sleep overcame her and she drifted into oblivion.

The harsh voices below wakened her. At first she was too dazed with sleep to understand what was happening or where she was. There was someone in the stable talking loudly as if drunk or wildly excited. Cautiously she peered down from her vantage point, able to see only dim figures below. A match was struck and a lamp lit and in the light Gwendolyn recognized Carl Perkins. Someone was lying in the dirt showing no signs of life, even when Perkins kicked him.

'Get the horses saddled up. We got to take this sumbitch Truman out into the canyons and dump him.'

Gwendolyn sucked in her breath: Perkins had taken his revenge on his enemy. A feeling of sadness swept over Gwendolyn as she realized Ben Truman was dead. She had been intrigued by the young outlaw and wondered at his inclusion in the Jones gang. From what she had heard and seen his actions were certainly not those of a hardened criminal.

'Good job that sheriff gave us the nod we had a spy in our camp. God knows what kind of trap this sumbitch might have led us into.'

They readied the horses, unaware they were being watched. Gwendolyn stared down at the body of Truman. She realized what had happened. Jones had been warned there was a plant inside his gang and the outlaw chief had fingered Truman. It looked as if the youngster was taking the rap for Gwendolyn. A knot of anger grew inside her as she watched the outlaws manhandle Trumans body onto the back of a horse and tie him in place.

'We'll need a fire. Find a sack while I grab a handful of logs from the heap here and plenty of straw to get it going. We can give Truman a lot more pain to send him on his way to hell.'

Gwendolyn tensed when she heard this. Truman wasn't dead, though by the state of his bloodied features it looked like he wasn't far off.

As the horses exited the livery, Gwendolyn hastily clambered down from her perch. Quickly she saddled up and began trailing the riders.

Ben Truman came to, draped across a horse. At first he was not aware of where he was or what had happened to him. All he was conscious of was the pain – excruciating pain – so intense it robbed him of the ability to think coherently. He tried to move, to ease some of his agony, but he was lashed securely to the horse. Memory came flooding back of the beating he had received at the hands of Carl Perkins while Ernest Jones interrogated him. Now he was being transported God knows where.

'This'll do.'

The horses stopped moving and the men dismounted. A hand grasped his hair and someone peered at him.

'Has he come to yet or has the sumbitch gone and died out of spite?'

'I think he's still alive.'

'Get him off the horse and prop him against that rock. Then we'll get the fire going.'

Ben was roughly hauled from the top of the horse and dumped in the dirt. He could not suppress a groan as he hit the ground.

'Ah, he's still alive. We'll have him squealing soon as we get the knife warmed in the fire.'

Flames leapt into the straw, licking round the logs and illuminating the scene. Perkins and his companion crouched over the fire, balancing the blade of a Bowie in the flames.

'A hot knife soon sets a man to howling. There's something enjoyable hearing a fella beg for mercy. I don't put the eyes out till last. I like 'em to see me as I work.'

The second man chortled then stood up from the fire.

'I got me a bottle in the saddle-bags.'

Out in the night Gwendolyn had managed to creep close to the men as they were engrossed in lighting the fire. She heard enough to understand what they were about to do. She felt sick with apprehension. The man the outlaws were about to torture was there in her place. She was the spy they were looking for and instead of tagging her they had cottoned on to Ben Truman. But for that mistake it would be her sitting against the rock awaiting the searing pain of a hot blade. She knew unless she did something Ben Truman would spend the night in screaming agony before Perkins finished him off. Slowly, she drew her pistol.

116

28

'OK, you fellas, shuck your irons and hands above your head.'

The men crouching by the fire looked up in consternation.

'What the—'

Slowly the men stood, staring out from the fire at the dim figure holding them at gunpoint.

'I said hands above your heads.'

'Who the hell are you?'

'Never mind that – just do as you're told. Any tricks an' I'll shoot both of you.'

Neither of the outlaws made any attempt to do as Gwendolyn told them. Imperceptibly they were edging apart from each other. Men like Perkins and his companion lived by bloodshed and conflict. When faced with danger their reaction was sudden and violent.

'Sure thing, we ain't wanting any bother, mister. We got a hurt fella here and we're aiming to fix him up some.'

Perkins turned and pointed at Ben. As he did so the two men dived apart, at the same time pulling their weapons. Out in the night Gwendolyn was caught unawares. From being in control with her gun on the outlaws she was suddenly in the path of a hail of lead as the gunmen fired at her. Gwendolyn fell flat and sent a couple of shots winging towards the nearest man.

When she confronted the outlaws she had been shaking with fright. She had never been in a situation like this and was ill-prepared for the sudden violence of her opponents. She felt a whisper of something past her head and realized the precariousness of her situation. Bullets were hitting around her and she knew she had to move. All her fright and nervousness fell away and she began calculating the odds of survival. She fired towards the gun flashes and rolled to a new position.

Gwendolyn noted the gun shots were coming from different positions as the gunmen moved into a new location after firing off a few shots. Unknown to her, Perkins and his companion were manoeuvring in a flanking movement to come from either side and make it harder for her to concentrate her fire on one or the other.

These men were veterans of many a gunfight and they played the game in a knowledge that their partner knew exactly how to react as the circumstances of the shootout changed. They had been held at gunpoint but now they had the upper hand and instead of being held at bay they were now stalking their attacker.

Gwendolyn tried to concentrate on the gun flashes but they kept moving as soon as she fired. Bullets were hitting all around her. At any moment one of the outlaws would get lucky and she would be hit and killed or maybe just wounded. The thought of this last situation chilled her. Instead of rescuing Ben Truman she would join him by the fire and both would be screaming as the outlaws worked on them with their knives.

'Toby, can you see the sumbitch?' Perkins called out.

'Sure Carl, I got him right in my sights. Do you want me to plug him?'

'Don't kill him outright. I want to hear him scream when I put that red-hot blade in his gizzard.'

This conversation only confirmed Gwendolyn's estimation of her dire situation. She reasoned also they were bluffing about having her under observation.

'Keep firing, I'm right behind the sumbitch.'

The shooting intensified and Gwendolyn had to keep her head down as lead bullets buzzed around her. Concealed in the rocks she rolled over on to her back and stared up at the night sky. She held the gun loosely across her chest and listened to the sounds around her. She was sure now of her strategy.

Lie possum and wait for one of the gunmen to stumble over her. As soon as she had him in her sights she would shoot. She forced herself to remain still, watching and listening intently for the gunmen moving on her position.

Ben could see the knife embedded in the glowing embers of the fire and began a painful crawl towards it. Each foot of ground was bought at a fearful cost of pain and effort. Flat on the earth he squirmed those few vital yards towards the flames and the weapon. The knife was not much against the six-guns blasting into the night but it was better than nothing.

Once the knife was retrieved he continued his painfully slow crawling. He had a target in mind. Ben figured he might distract or even disable one of the outlaws and give his rescuer, whoever he was, a better chance of surviving.

On he inched, each movement a painful battle fought against weakness and debilitating pain. He heard the shouting but there was no response from the man who had intervened. Perhaps he was lying out there badly wounded or even dead. No matter, Ben was dead anyway, he just had to try and take out one or other of the outlaws that were intent on killing him in a most painful manner.

The gun flashes were closer now. The knife was held fast in Ben's fist, the blade jutting up in the air, the tip dull red now that it was removed from the fire and beginning to cool. Any slight noise he might have made was masked by the thunder of gunfire.

Ben saw the shape of the man lying on the ground out-lined against the muzzle flash and knew his task was almost done. He forced himself to his hands and knees and moved the remaining few feet towards his victim. The gunman was concentrating on the last place he had seen the intruder and took no notice of anything behind him. In one last des-perate effort Ben sprawled on top of his victim.

The outlaw was taken completely by surprise. Before he could react Ben plunged the glowing tip of the knife into the man's neck just below his ear. The injured man opened his mouth to scream and at the same time Ben twisted the Bowie and pushed harder, trying to do as much damage as he could before his strength failed him. His victim was making strangled noises as the big blade penetrated his head, rupturing blood vessels and severing nerves.

Ben sprawled on the gunman's back, desperately twisting and pushing the handle of the knife, which was becoming slippery with blood. Beneath him the stricken man jerked and shuddered as the hot steel hacked at his brain. And then the heaving stopped and the gunman subsided with a long and eerie groan. Still Ben rammed the steel and shoved till his arm gave out and he was forced to cease his deadly actions.

Ben rolled on to the dirt and reached for the dead man's gun. There was sporadic gunfire from out in the night. He fired a few shots from his newly acquired weapon, hoping to fool the second outlaw into believing he still had his partner's support in his hunt for the unknown attacker.

He found the gunbelt stuffed with spare cartridges and, slowly and painfully, reloaded. Now he was armed but he was weak and near collapse. He began the painful journey back towards the fire.

29

Gwendolyn heard the crunching of rock on rock and turned to face the sound. She scanned the place she thought she heard the clatter but could see nothing. She kept her gun aimed in that direction so did not see the figure rise out of the darkness and drop down behind her. A gun barrel was pushed into her neck.

'As much as twitch and your brains will be splattered from here to town,' the voice of Carl Perkins told her, and then in a louder voice, 'Toby, I got the sumbitch.' A hand reached over, took her gun and tossed it away. 'I threw a rock over there and had you aiming at a ghost. Simple but effective. On your feet.'

Gwendolyn slowly rose and her captor gave a grunt of surprise.

'Goddamnit, Caruthers. What's your game?'

She did not reply and Perkins gave her a violent shove that almost tumbled her to the dirt again.

'Walk towards the fire.'

Gwendolyn stumbled in the direction of the camp-fire. They got there without any response from the second gunman. Gwendolyn stared soberly at Ben, still slumped where he had been dropped.

'I'm sorry, fella,' she said.

The young outlaw made no response.

'Toby,' Perkins yelled. 'Where the hell are you?'

Suddenly he swung his pistol and caught Gwendolyn on the side of the head. The blow caught her with such force she staggered and went down.

'If you killed Toby you'll suffer, you sumbitch. Toby, where the hell are you?'

There was no response and Perkins kicked Gwendolyn. He levelled his pistol, his hand shaking as rage overcame him.

'I ought to kill you. But I got a better idea.' Perkins stuffed his pistol back in his holster and turned towards the fire. 'Goddamn knife, where's that goddamn knife?'

Ben tried to hold the pistol steady. It seemed too heavy for his hand. He raised his other arm and rested the barrel across it. He fired and hit Perkins in the buttock. Perkins yelled. His leg gave way and he knelt in the fire scattering faggots and sparks.

'Goddamn—'

Ben fired again and this time his bullet went into the outlaw's back. Perkins pitched forward across the camp-fire and started to scream as the flames licked at his clothing. He tried to roll away from the blaze but the bullet in his back had damaged his spine and he was finding it difficult to move. He kept screaming and clawing at the dirt as the flames licked hungrily at his clothes.

Gwendolyn grabbed Perkins by the boots and began hauling him out of the fire. She dragged him clear but his shirt was ablaze and she looked round for something to douse the flames. In desperation, she yanked off her jacket and threw it across the blaze. Smoke and the smell of burning flesh rose from the wounded man. He was moaning loudly, alternately cursing and screaming. Gwendolyn watched helplessly. She was more terrified now than when she was out in the rocks being shot at.

'Ben, what'll we do?'

'What can we do? The bastard's done for.'

'We can't leave him like this. We got to take him into town

and have someone patch him up.'

'You crazy? As soon as I show up back there they'll finish what they started. I won't survive and you won't either when Perkins tells them what happened.'

Perkins was moaning pitifully; smoke was still rising from his charred clothing.

'Best thing is to put him out of his misery with a bullet in the head. Here, take this pistol and do it.'

Gwendolyn recoiled from the proffered weapon.

'What . . . you . . . we can't do that . . . just kill him.'

'What the hell you think he was going to do to us? Look at the state of me. Perkins was happily beating the hell out of me back in Drygulch. Jones told him to take me outside the town and bury me. He had a knife in the fire heating it so as he could torture me some more.'

Gwendolyn shuddered. 'I know what you're saying is true but we just can't kill him in cold blood.'

'One of us has to. I guess it'll have to be me.'

Ben got to his hands and knees and crawled over to the moaning figure of Perkins.

'Wait, maybe he wants to say a prayer or something.'

'Jeez, are you serious? He's a heartless, vicious killer. You think a prayer is going to help him any?'

Gwendolyn ignored Truman and knelt beside Perkins. She almost retched as the smoky fumes rose from his charred body.

'Carl, I . . . we . . . do you want to say a prayer or any-thing?'

Perkins began to curse and swear. 'Kill me . . . just kill me . . . I can't stand it anymore.'

Gwendolyn was petrified thinking of what had to be done but she stayed kneeling.

'Dear God, please don't be too hard on Carl here. He had a hard life—'

She was interrupted by a scream from Perkins. 'Do it! Just kill me for God's sake!'

Gwendolyn scrambled away and went over to where the outlaws' horses were standing. She didn't look back. She reached out and stroked the nearest horse. When the shot came she rested her head against the horse's neck and felt the tears running down her cheeks.

'It's done,' Ben called.

The young outlaw was slumped beside the body of Perkins. Trying to avoid looking at the dead outlaw, Gwendolyn came back to the fire.

'Goddamnit, I ain't worth a spit,' Ben said at last.

Even in the poor light from the dying fire Gwendolyn could see Ben looked terrible. His face was swollen and smeared with blood.

'Was it bad?'

'They tied me to a chair and Perkins beat me. Jones kept asking me the same stupid damned questions: Who was I spying for? How was I to contact them? He obviously mistook me for someone else. When I passed out they threw water on me and started all over again.

'That seems to be the story of my life. I get punished for something other people do. I hope they catch that goddamn spy and roast him just like Perkins was going to do to me. Damn him and them both to hell.' Ben fell silent musing on the quirks of fate that that had blighted his life. 'Well, I sure ain't their spy. Jones kept talking about this sheriff as had sent him word of the spy. Don't surprise me none. Being a lawman doesn't mean you're honest and square.'

'Sheriff? Did they say a name?'

'Sure did. Tom Malloy or some such.'

'Tomalley, Sheriff Tomalley.'

'You know him?'

'Yeah. He's sheriff of Fullerton. So that's why Jones knew

where Blatch lived. We figured they sassed out the town afore the robbery. But Tomalley must have told Jones about the bank and how to go about it.'

Ben was staring at Gwendolyn. 'You!' he hissed. 'You're the goddamn spy.' He was still holding the gun. Now he brought it up and pointed it at Gwendolyn. 'I ought to blow your blasted brains out.'

Gwendolyn stared down at the gun within reaching distance and for a moment wondered if she could make a grab for it. It was obvious the young outlaw was in a bad way. She might just be able to wrest the weapon from him. As she tensed for action the barrel of the gun dropped.

'Hell, in spite of all that, you saved my life when you came out here after me. I guess I owe you. But when I'm fit again I'm going to beat the living daylights out of you.'

'What now?'

'We can't stay out here, that's for sure. When Jones finds Perkins and his pard, he'll come looking for me. I need to rest up an' regain my strength afore I make a break for it. I'm bust up pretty bad.'

'Can you sit a horse?'

Ben shook his head. 'I ain't fit to ride no distance. I'll have to find a hideout somewhere nearby.'

'I bin thinking. What if I take you back to town? Hide you in the livery.'

'You could do that?'

'If I can get you back under cover of darkness and sneak you in the livery, no one need ever know you're there.'

30

Once Gwendolyn had Ben safely hidden, weariness overcame her and she settled down to catch up on some much needed sleep. The shouting from below awakened her and for a moment she panicked, thinking her secret had been discovered. Light was filtering into the livery and she suddenly realized it was morning.

'Glen! Where in tarnation is that damned helper. Glen!'

'Here, Mr Worth.'

Gwendolyn scrambled down while being berated by her new boss.

'Is that what I pay you for – to sleep all day?'

'Sorry, Mr Worth. I guess I slept in. All that hard work I put in yesterday plumb wore me out.'

'Hard work! Young 'uns nowadays don't know what work is. Get this place cleaned up and swept and the water casks filled up. I'll be in the office doing the accounts.'

Grumbling as he stomped away, the livery owner disappeared into the small room at the back that he called his office and slammed the door behind him. Once inside he put his feet up on the battered desk and began to doze.

Partway through her tasks Gwendolyn heard the commotion and went to the door of the livery. Along the street came a procession of horses. Two of them carried bodies draped over the saddles.

'What happened?' someone called.

'It's Carl Perkins and his buddy, Toby Rankin,' the leading rider yelled back.

The horsemen pulled up outside the Death's Head Saloon. A crowd was gathering and Gwendolyn joined them. She pushed forward and reached the front just as Ernest Jones come out on the boardwalk. He stepped down to the horses. All around her she could hear murmuring as people speculated on the cause of death.

'Could be Injuns. See the burns.'

Jones looked up at the men who had brought in the bodies.

'Where'd you find them?'

'Just out of town. Noticed the buzzards and went to have a look-see.'

'No sign of anyone else?'

'Nary a sign. There was a burnt-out fire. I reckon someone roasted Perkins over that fire – someone with a grudge against him.'

Ernest Jones turned and faced the crowd of onlookers.

'Last night I found out we had a snake amongst us – a lawman posing as one of us.' There was a rumbling from the crowd. 'It was Ben Truman, who we busted out of the penitentiary. We tried to get him to talk but he wouldn't tell us who he was working for. No matter. I sent these two out to finish him off and bury the body in the canyon. Truman was in a bad way. By the time we'd finished with him he weren't fit to take on Carl and Toby. He must have had help. I want to know who helped him. Anyone knows anything speak up. We got to catch whoever did this.'

There was a lot of muttering amongst the crowd but no one came forward with anything useful.

'I'm offering $100 for anyone as turns them in.'

That did create a buzz.

'Truman won't get far. I'm forming a search party. We'll gather here in ten minutes. I need every man as can fork a horse to ride with me. We can spread out and hunt down that son of a bitch.'

Gwendolyn drifted back to the livery and climbed the ladder to the hayloft.

'They just brought in the bodies,' she whispered. There was no reply. 'Jones is forming a search party.' There was still no response. 'Jones offered $100 reward. I'm just going over to the Death's Head to collect.'

A head adorned with wisps of hay appeared.

'What'd you say?'

'They're forming a search party to look for you. How are you feeling? And keep your voice down. The livery owner's out back.'

'I feel as if I've been on the receiving end of a stampede and every cow in the herd stamped me.' Ben's face was puffed, his swollen eyes were almost closed and dried blood soiled what was visible of his skin. 'If I look as bad as I feel I'd rather you didn't tell me.'

'You have to get out of Drygulch Canyon some way or other. For now just stay low.'

'I need a drink.'

Gwendolyn found a canteen and filled it with water and took it up to Ben.

'Bourbon?'

'Yeah, though I mixed water with it. I didn't want you getting drunk and falling out of the tree.'

Ben took a slug from the canteen and screwed up his battered face.

'Ugh, water! I need something stronger if I'm to recover.'

'Yeah, well just lie low for now. I got to do some work an' keep that old coot from giving me the sack.'

Gwendolyn worked steadily at the livery cleaning out stalls, renewing straw, filling hay feeders and water butts and sweeping out the yard. All the while her brain was churning as she tried to figure out a way to get Ben Truman out of

Drygulch. Midmorning Ted Worth came out to see how she was faring.

'Gawd almighty, this place is a midden. If Joseph and Mary were to come here they wouldn't even put their mule inside never mind bed down for the night.'

A hot retort was on Gwendolyn's lips but she bit it back. She was holding the broom at the time and had an overpowering urge to take it and ram it up the old-timer's backside.

'I would think Drygulch Canyon is the last place the Holy couple would want to come to. I got to take a break for some breakfast. I ain't had a bite since last night.'

'Humph! You got any money?' The livery owner dug into his pocket and to Gwendolyn's surprise, pulled out a couple of crumpled dollar bills. 'I guess I owe you a day's wages.' He thrust the notes at Gwendolyn, turned and stomped back to his office. 'An' don't take all day. I want this place fixed up proper, ya hear?'

Gwendolyn stared at the retreating back. Two dollars was more than she expected. In fact, she assumed Worth would pay her by allowing her to sleep in the livery. She began to suspect the old grouch was really not a bad sort and hid his good nature behind his tetchy demeanour.

'Thank you, Mr Worth,' she called, and got an impatient wave in return before he disappeared into his retreat.

Gwendolyn headed down to the Death's Head. She had two objectives: Ben had requested bourbon and they both needed food.

31

The Death's Head Saloon was quiet with just a handful of drinkers and a poker game going on at one of the tables. Many of the inhabitants of Drygulch were out scouring the canyon for Ben Truman. Gwendolyn went to the bar and before she could order, saw the barman was preparing a tray of food.

'How'd you know I was coming in?' she quipped. 'I'm so hungry I could eat the hind leg of a mangy dog fried in sarsaparilla.'

'Howdy, young fella. This is spoken for. Say, you could do me a favour. Deliver this to room seven upstairs. We have a special guest staying. An' when you come back I'll have something ready for you.'

'Sure thing.' Gwendolyn picked up the tray.

'You'll need this.' The barkeep placed a key on the tray. 'Make sure you lock up after.'

Thoughtfully Gwendolyn mounted the stairs. She unlocked the door and stepped inside. Handcuffed to a bed across the room was a young woman.

'Howdy, miss. Breakfast.'

The girl glared sullenly at her. 'When are you going to let me go?'

Gwendolyn's heart was beating fast. She suspected this was the young woman she had vowed to rescue. She put the tray on the bed.

'What's your name?'

'Alice Salinger. Who wants to know? And take that

130

horrible food away. I'm not eating anything till you free me.'

Gwendolyn sat on the bed. 'Alice, listen to me. I've been sent here to rescue you.'

Alice sat up, her eyes brightening. 'Oh thank God. I was giving up hope. Are you taking me out now?' The words tumbled out excitedly.

'Alice, it's not that easy. We need a plan. Do they ever release you from those cuffs?'

'When I go to the john, they release me then.'

'Is there a regular time you go? If I know you're out of the cuffs and out of the room that's the best time to strike. Tell me exactly what happens.'

Gwendolyn returned to the livery carrying a bundle of food and climbed to the loft.

'Pssst, I brought you some grub.'

The fugitive crawled over and she handed him the package. Opening it, Ben discovered a bottle of bourbon, half a loaf and a slab of roast pork. He tackled the bourbon first.

'Aaah,' he gasped, 'that's the second time you saved my life.' Eagerly he bit into the pork. 'Any thoughts on how we going to get out of this hellhole?'

Gwendolyn decided not to tell Ben about the added complication of Alice.

'I'm working on it. They've got lookouts on the passes.'

Ben stopped chewing for a moment. 'Hell, I don't want to spend the rest of my life in a hayloft!'

'It mightn't be that bad. I heard about hermits that live isolated in caves. They were saintly men and became closer to God by cutting themselves off from the temptations of the world.'

'Yeah, well if I don't get out of here, Ernest Jones will be cutting something off me and sending me to meet God sooner than I want to.'

Gwendolyn couldn't help but giggle at Ben's response. Ben grinned back at her. He liked this sparky young fella who had saved him from Perkins and a hideous death. Hearing noises below, Gwendolyn quickly descended just in time to be caught working by the livery owner.

'I suppose you been idling your time while I been busy in the office,' he grumbled. 'Sleeping on the job, more than likely.' He gazed round at the tidy stables with horses contentedly munching hay in stables with fresh straw and well-filled water butts. 'We're low on supplies. Looks like I got to make a trip outside the canyon.' Grumbling, the oldster turned away. 'Don't let me catch you shirking again. There's plenty as would be glad of your job.' Suddenly he stopped. 'Say, young'un, can you drive a wagon?'

'Sure thing. I was a teamster afore coming here,' Gwendolyn boasted. 'Drove freight for Fargo.'

'A teamster, haw, haw, haw,' the old-timer chortled. 'Would this veteran teamster be capable of driving a wagon to Coyote Junction, pick up a load of supplies an' bring it back in one piece?'

'Sure thing. I know Coyote Junction like the back of my hand. Be there an' back afore you can say, "holy cow, what kept you".'

Worth looked suspiciously at his helper thinking his last remark held more meaning than he let on, but Gwendolyn was innocuously sweeping non-existent wisps of hay from the walkway.

'Humph, I'll get a list together. You can start in the morning.' He moved away then turned back. 'Can I trust you with the money? You'll have to pay for the supplies.'

'Mr Worth, you've been good to me giving me a job an' a place to sleep. I ain't never going to steal from you.'

But as she said it Gwendolyn wondered, if things went according to plan, would the livery owner ever get his wagon back? Her mind was working overtime as she weighed up the prospects of using the livery vehicle as a means of escape from Drygulch Canyon.

32

The wagon was hitched up and ready. Gwendolyn was edgy as the livery owner hovered about watching her as she made preparations for the trip. The previous night she had discussed the plan with Ben. He had been incredulous when she broached the idea of rescuing Alice Salinger.

'Dad blasted, I forgot all about her. I remember Jones taking her along when we ran from Fullerton. How you going to get her out of the saloon?'

'She's handcuffed to the bed but they release her to go to the john. That's when I have to make my move.'

'It's dicey, Glen. I don't like the idea of you risking being caught. You're the only one they don't suspect. Without you the whole plan fails.'

'I can't leave her. If I don't get her out now there'll never be another chance.'

In the end Ben had reached out and taken Gwendolyn's hand in his.

'Glen, you're a fella as a man could ride the hills with. I know you have to do this for that poor gal. You've saved my life several times over, hiding me out here and all. I only wish I could come with you and help but as soon as I'm spotted the game's up.'

Gwendolyn felt a wave of light-headedness come over her

as Ben spoke to her and held her hand. Something crumbled inside and she wanted him to throw his arms around her and hold her close. She wanted to climb in the wagon and take him away to safety and to hell with everything else. It was a wave of emotion such as she had never felt before, and it was with great effort that she suppressed the feeling.

As far as Ben was concerned she was Glen Caruthers, a law officer, and she had to stay in that guise. Ernest Jones and his gang had taken away all dignity and respect that any man ought to expect from a woman. Gwendolyn Caruthers, the woman, had been ruined and no man would ever want to be associated with her. She would do her best to save Ben and Alice and if she managed that she would ride out of their lives.

The livery owner instructed Gwendolyn as she prepared the wagon for her trip. There were tarpaulins folded in the body of the wagon to cover the hay and anything else to be brought back from Coyote Junction.

'I guess I'd better go down the Death's Head and have some breakfast,' she said to Worth. 'I'm so hungry I could eat a horse's backside, tail an' all.'

This wasn't true for she had a lump of dread in her stomach and knew she would be incapable of eating anything.

'Doggone young'uns,' Worth said disgustedly. 'Eat, eat, eat. Whar the hell you put it all I'll never know. If you have to go then bring me back a bottle.'

Gwendolyn hurried down the street to the saloon. The barman greeted her with some friendliness. He was intrigued by the skinny youngster. She ate a hearty meal and then bought extra to take with her.

'Can I just have some fatback and bread? And wrap it for me; I got to take a wagon out for Ted Worth. Put a bottle of bourbon with that. I'm going outside – could you have it ready for me when I come in again.'

Gwendolyn went to the rear of the saloon and into the yard. This was where Alice was taken to make the call of nature. There were a couple of latrines made of boards with ill-fitting doors. A stairway ran up the back of the building to service the upper storey. There was a scraping noise from above and then the sound of someone descending.

Gwendolyn's insides were trembling with nerves. She wanted to be sick and looked round for somewhere to vomit then she leaned against the fencing screening the yard. Footsteps clattered on the wooden stairs behind her. Gwendolyn groaned loudly.

'Goddamn kids, can't hold their whiskey,' a man's voice said scornfully.

'Oh, the poor man. Let me help.'

'Stay back, miss. Just do what you have to do and let's get back upstairs again.'

Gwendolyn turned and rushed towards the wooden latrines. She was holding her hand over her mouth and making gulping noises.

'Goddamn—'

Alice's guard tried to step out of the way stumbling slightly in his haste. Gwendolyn cannoned into him and he lost his balance and went down. Even as he was falling Gwendolyn was drawing her pistol. Before he could react she cracked him across the temple.

'Aaaargh. . . .'

Gwendolyn swung again but the guard managed to block the blow and grabbed the weapon.

'I'm going to kill you for that.'

For moments they struggled for control of the gun. He was a strong man and suddenly wrenched the gun from Gwendolyn's hand while at the same time punching her in the face. She fell away from him and he quickly sat up with the captured gun in his hand.

'You goddamn bastard!' he yelled and pulled the trigger.

Nothing happened. When Gwendolyn lost her own weapon in the gunfight with Perkins she had taken his but never checked the loads. That oversight now saved her life. With a curse the guard flung the gun at Gwendolyn and pulled his own weapon.

'This one works,' he yelled.

Gwendolyn stared in fear at the gun aimed only feet away. There was no way the gunman could miss.

There was a sudden flurry of movement and something heavy hit the outlaw on top of his head. His eyes went glassy, the gun sagging in his grip. Alice raised the log she had pulled from the woodpile and smashed it once more on the guard's head. Such was the force of the blow his neck sunk into his shoulders and he subsided without another sound. For stunned moments the two women stared at each other.

'Quick,' Gwendolyn gasped, 'give me a hand to get him in the john.'

Between them they crammed the unconscious guard inside the latrine and pushed the door closed. He was so limp Gwendolyn wondered momentarily if he were dead. She unlatched the gate and peered out into a back alley.

'Walk along with me,' she told Alice. 'Just walk and talk. Don't run or hurry.'

They reached the street and walked along without too many curious glances. It was only as they came near the livery Gwendolyn remembered the food and the bourbon she had ordered.

'Damn, no matter,' she muttered. 'Slide in under there,' she ordered the girl and pulled the tarpaulin aside.

An anxious face peered out at them. Alice gasped and stepped back.

'It's all right, it's only Ben. He's going too.'

When she pulled the tarpaulin over the two figures it looked suspiciously bulky but there was no time to worry about that. Gwendolyn quickly jumped into the driver's seat and used the whip to flick across their rumps.

'Get up there, you bag of bones!' she yelled.

The horses obediently took off at a trot. Gwendolyn was so busy holding the reins and staying on the bouncing wagon seat she did not see the livery boss run out into the street and yell after her, wanting to know where the hell his bourbon was. Once out of the town Gwendolyn managed to slow the team and stop. She climbed down and walked to the rear of the vehicle.

'You two in the back, how are you?'

The tarpaulin lifted and two bemused faces peered out at Gwendolyn.

'What's happening?'

'We're clear of town; all we got to do now is get through the pass.'

'Well, try and drive a mite easier. We bounced around in here so much I got bruises on top of my other bruises.'

'Why don't you come round here and drive the damn wagon.'

'No, I don't think so.' Ben winked at Gwendolyn. 'I'm needed back here to protect this fair maiden.'

Alice blushed at his remark and for no reason she could think of Gwendolyn felt a stab of jealousy. Abruptly she jerked the tarpaulin back into place and heard Ben curse as his head bumped on the floor of the wagon. She couldn't hear his muffled remark.

'Just lay still and not a sound out of either of you. Don't move or speak until I say it is safe to do so.'

Back in the driving seat she set course for the pass that would take her out of Drygulch Canyon and to safety.

33

Gwendolyn's heart missed a beat as she saw the riders on the trail. And then the bottom dropped out of her stomach as she recognized Ernest Jones. The riders pulled up blocking the trail so Gwendolyn had to draw to a halt.

'Howdy,' she called, 'you catch that lowdown renegade yet?'

Jones nudged his mount forward. 'What you doing out here?'

'Mister Worth sent me to fetch supplies. I'm on my way to Coyote Crossing.'

The outlaw chief was frowning as he stared at Gwendolyn. She tried to keep her face composed but her insides were churning.

'That lowdown traitor Truman doing that to poor Carl,' she said. 'Perkins was a mean bastard but he didn't deserve to have that done to him.'

'Yeah, well we'll get that son of a bitch sooner or later and he'll suffer worse than Perkins. Truman is still out here somewhere. He can't get out of the canyon with men posted in the pass. I got searchers all over looking. If you spot him just shoot. Don't take any chances.'

'You bet; I owe him one for Carl.'

Jones was staring intently at Gwendolyn. Casually she reached for her holstered gun and with bewildering speed Jones had his pistol out and aimed at her. Gwendolyn's eyes opened wide and immediately shoved her hands in the air.

'W-what's the matter?' She stuttered seeing death in the

outlaw's eyes.

'Don't ever go for you gun while you're with me, sonny.'

'I . . . you . . . you said as Truman was still out there. I was just making sure my gun was loaded an' ready.'

Beniah Arnold burst out laughing. 'Ernest, I reckon that kid will need a change of pants, you scared him so bad.'

Someone else chortled and as the merriment grew it eventually affected Jones. A slow grin spread across his face.

'I reckon.' He suddenly roared with laughter. 'You'd better pull off the trail and clean yourself up, kid.'

'Careful you don't pick up a cactus to wipe with,' Gibbons yelled. 'You can get a nasty prick from one of them.'

It was a light relief from the tense hours of hunting and the outlaws loosened up as they ribbed the nervous youngster on the wagon. Still chuckling the outlaws filed past each side of the wagon and continued on their merry way.

Gwendolyn sat trembling on the wagon seat, listening to the movement of horses as the outlaws rode away. She was afraid to turn around in case she would see Jones and his gang circling back.

'Gee up there.'

The team obediently leaned into the traces and the wagon began to rumble forward. The one thing she was grateful for was the complete absence of any movement or noise from the back where Ben and Alice were hiding.

On the wagon rumbled and Gwendolyn could not shake off the feeling the outlaws would come racing up and shoot her and the wagon to pieces. She was afraid to communicate with her companions in case someone was watching and so she drove the wagon forward and approached the pass guarded by men with orders not to let anyone out of the canyon who had not a good reason for leaving.

'Halt!'

The sudden shout startled Gwendolyn and she jerked on

the reins stopping their forward motion. A man holding a rifle stepped out from behind a cluster of rocks and stood observing her.

'Howdy fella. Where you heading?'

'Hell, I just went through all that with Ernest. The wagon belongs to Ted Worth at the livery. I'm on my way to Coyote Crossing for supplies. If you're still here when I come back I'll bring you a bag of candies.'

'You met up with Jones? He catch up with the fella as killed Toby and Carl?'

'Not yet. But Ernest reckons he won't get far. He'll have to get past you fellas first.'

'That's right. Jones says as I was to search all wagons and question anyone as was coming in or out. I'll just take a look back there.'

'Hell, it's just old rolled up tarps.'

'No matter, I still got to look.'

'Say, who else is up here with you? Can a fella get a job doing what you're doing?'

'Johnny Durango is up on the top there, and on the other side is Pete Smalley. Why the hell you want a job like this? Boring as hell and dry too. Jones don't allow no drinking on guard duty.' The outlaw was moving to the back of the wagon.

'Hell, fella, I'm late as it is. I don't want to stay overnight in Coyote Crossing. Can I go now?'

'Not afore I take a look-see.'

Gwendolyn was slipping her pistol from the holster. It looked like they were rumbled. The guard pulled back the tarpaulin and stared down at Ben Truman with a pistol in his hand.

'What the. . . !'

'OK, fella, just toss that rifle into the back of the wagon and any other weapons you might be carrying.'

'Shit, you son of a bitch.'

'Do it, fella. I killed Perkins and his pal Toby. I'll just as soon kill you as be caught by Jones.'

It was a mistake to mention Jones. He was a ruthless leader who punished mercilessly any of his gang who failed him. The guard knew if he didn't stop the wagon then he would receive harsh justice from the outlaw chief.

'Don't shoot; I'll do as you say.'

But even as he spoke he raised the rifle and swung it down towards Ben while at the same time squeezing trigger.

One of the attractions of Drygulch Canyon as a hideout for the outlaws was its tendency to magnify sounds, which travelled into the surrounding locality. This had the effect of creating an early warning system for the outlaws hiding out in the canyon.

The shooting at the entrance echoed back down the trail and reached the ears of Ernest Jones and his band of men jogging back towards town for refreshments before resuming the hunt for Ben Truman.

'Trouble at the pass,' Jones yelled and swung his mount around.

34

Ben flinched as the rifle went off. The shot went into the floor of the wagon and Ben instinctively fired. The rifleman disappeared from view and Ben wasn't sure if he had hit him. He did not have time to wonder for the wagon lurched forward as the shots spooked the horses.

Gwendolyn made no attempt to stop the wagon. Whatever was happening behind her she knew she had to keep going. Suddenly more shots rang out and bullets thudded into the body of the wagon as the watchers on the heights joined in the shooting. There was no option but to keep going and trust to luck to get past the marksmen unscathed.

'Shoot back at those sons of bitches!' she yelled but wasn't sure anyone heard her above the clatter of the wagon and the shooting.

She grabbed up the whip and began to lash the poor horses even though they were running scared and nothing she was doing would get more speed out of them.

The occasional bullet thudded into the wagon. Gwendolyn began to worry a horse would be hit and that would be the end of their escape bid. On they went and the firing became more irregular with less lead hitting the wagon. And then they were out in the open and the firing ceased altogether. She nearly jumped out of the wagon when she felt a hand on her shoulder and a voice shouting in her ear.

'Keep going, Glen. I reckon we're clear.'

'Keep an eye on our backtrail. Jones wasn't that far away when the shooting started. He's bound to hear and come running,' she yelled.

On they thundered on the uneven trail. As well as worrying about Jones coming after them, Gwendolyn was concerned something might happen to the wagon. They were haring along at breakneck speed with the wagon bouncing and heaving beneath her. A broken wheel or a lame horse would slow them down or stop them completely and then they would be at the mercy of Jones once he caught up with them.

Ben was kneeling by the tailgate when he saw the horsemen appear out of the dust kicked up by the careering wagon.

'Goddamn, we got the Devil up our ass,' he muttered. He turned and grinned at Alice sitting up and holding on to the side of the wagon. 'See if you can borrow a gun from Glen,' he yelled. 'Maybe we can shoot a few afore they catch us.'

She nodded and turned to crawl up to the front. Ben turned to the rear again and groaned. The trail seemed to be filled with horsemen. It looked like all the men out searching for the fugitive had heard the shooting and converged on the pass.

'Jeez, all I ever wanted was a quiet life.'

He checked the loads in his gun and settled down to wait. Carrying Gwendolyn's Colt, Alice crawled to crouch beside Ben.

'Don't do any shooting till they get closer and don't worry about hitting anything. Just aim in the general direction. With all this jolting about it'll be hard to hit a target. With luck we might hit one or two and that'll discourage the rest.'

But Ben did not believe that. Jones would run them till the horses dropped or they were shot from the wagon one by one. Of the two possibilities he favoured the second. He did not relish the though of falling into Jones's hands again. He'd already had a taste of what that entailed and it seemed to Ben a quick death from a bullet would be preferable to an agonizing death over a slow fire.

The wagon swerved and bounced wildly as Gwendolyn tried to guide the horses past potholes and boulders on the rough track. It was hardly fit to be called a track. The outlaws were wary of leaving a trail that might be followed and came and went by different ways. As the wagon swerved about, the dust thrown up by the wheels swirled and cleared slightly. Ben drew in a sharp breath as he saw again the horde of horsemen riding in pursuit.

'Damnation, it looks like Jones has roped in every gunhand in Drygulch.' He turned and grimaced at Alice clutching her Colt and squinting into the dust. 'What do you think, Miss Alice? We more than a match for them no-good outlaws?'

To Ben's bemusement the girl grinned back at him, her teeth showing up very white against the dust coating her face. Just then he felt something pass in the air and ducked his head. He peered out at the pursuers.

'Goddamn, they're getting close.'

Ben aimed his pistol over the tailgate and loosed off a shot. It did not have any effect. Beside him Alice fired her weapon. The battle of Drygulch Canyon had begun and there could be only one outcome. There were upwards of thirty or so bandits in pursuit of the three fugitives. The odds were all in the bandits' favour.

Ben fired again and beside him Alice matched him shot for shot. Bullets thudded into the rear of the wagon and some buzzed past them. Undeterred, they fired shot after shot at the massed horde of outlaws. A horse went down and spilled its rider. The effect was spectacular. The following riders tried to avoid the spill without success and three more horses went down.

'Whoopee! Good shooting, Alice.'

The pace of the pursuers slowed as the couple in the wagon fired more shots at the horde of riders. In a while Ben realized the distance between wagon and horsemen was increasing and he had hope they had discouraged the outlaws from further pursuit.

For a time they continued like this with the outlaws holding a steady pace and keeping out of shooting range. But then Ben suddenly realized that Jones had changed tactics. Instead of running them down, he was content to pace the horses and wait till their quarry tired and then he would close in for the kill. Time was on the outlaws' side. The prairie stretched out, mile after featureless mile. There was no refuge within a couple of days' ride.

'Stop shooting,' he told Alice. She looked at him quizzically. 'They're keeping their distance.'

All day the chase went on; the horses pulling the wagon tiring now. They had lasted well because they were drawing an empty wagon. But the relentless pace was beginning to take its toll and the animals were slowing. Gwendolyn knew she could not keep the team going for much longer without a break.

With this in mind she scanned the terrain looking for something that might give them a small advantage. In the distance she saw a mound rising from the flat landscape. As they drew nearer Gwendolyn realized the knoll she mistook for a hill was in fact a cluster of trees; and with that realization she knew exactly where she was. This was Little Buffalo waterhole where Harold Quigley and his posse had perished.

All roads lead here, she thought.

Gwendolyn altered course towards the trees. This is where fate had led them and this is where they would stop and hold Ernest Jones at bay till their ammo ran out or the outlaw gang overwhelmed them.

Gwendolyn drove the wagon around the grove of trees till they were out of sight of the outlaw gang. She gave a sharp pull on the reins to guide the outfit into the trees. All her attention was on making this manoeuvre so she did not see what she was driving into till too late.

With sudden shock she stared with mounting dread at the dozens of rifles aimed at the wagon. Jones had obviously anticipated their destination and sent men ahead to wait for them. Gwendolyn reached for her gun. Ben had the same thought but stopped when the harsh command barked out at them.

'Don't be foolish.'

The man who spoke was of squat build with a handlebar moustache. He wore a derby and a dustcoat. He looked mean and ready to use the Remington repeater he was aiming at Gwendolyn. The youngsters in the wagon stopped moving; it was hopeless anyway. Behind the speaker were more rifles all aimed at the wagon. The amount of firepower was overwhelming.

35

Gwendolyn looked over at her two companions. 'I'm so sorry . . .' she began, when a sudden shout interrupted her.

'Glen, what in goddamn hell?'

Gwendolyn looked up in bewilderment as Sheriff Humphrey Quigley came striding over.

'Grimes, put up that rifle. I know this fella.'

'Sheriff Quigley, what are you doing here?'

There was another shock as Nathaniel Shaler appeared behind Quigley.

'Glen, am I glad to see you. What's happening?'

'Nathaniel . . . I brought you a little surprise. If you look over in that direction,' Gwendolyn pointed with her whip, 'you'll see a band of riders. Ernest Jones is on his way with his gang of hellions. He wants to take me and Ben and Alice back to Drygulch Canyon.'

All heads swivelled as the men with the guns turned in the direction Gwendolyn was pointing. They rushed to the trees and peered out at the approaching horsemen.

'By God! Jones, you say? OK, men, maybe this is where we

put an end to Ernest Jones and his gang once and for all. Take cover in the trees.'

Nathanial Shaler was taking charge and the waterhole became a hive of activity as armed men ran to take up position. Some crouched down behind trees while others leaned against tree trunks, all grim-looking men with rifles which moments before had been aimed at Gwendolyn and her companions. Sheriff Quigley grinned up at Gwendolyn.

'You goddamn son of a bitch, I was sure I'd never see you again. In the end I persuaded Shaler to bring his men out here in the hope we might find some way of getting inside Drygulch.

'You better get down off that wagon afore the fireworks start.' The sheriff noticed Alice then. 'Glen, don't tell me this is Alice Salinger, the gal you went to rescue.'

'Sure is, Sheriff,' Alice piped up. 'Glen is a real hero. He saved me and Ben Truman here.'

Any further conversation was cut short when they heard Shaler shouting instructions to his men.

'Come on,' Sheriff Quigley said. 'Get under cover afore the action starts.'

Quickly, Gwendolyn clambered down from the wagon and followed Sheriff Quigley to the cover of the trees. She felt someone crowd in close beside her. It was Alice. She was smiling at Gwendolyn.

'I'm staying close to you, Glen. I feel safe with you around.'

Gwendolyn did not have time to reply. Shaler was calling out last minute instructions to the men.

'Remember, you got to let them get in real close. Aim for body shots. If the men don't go down then shoot the goddamn horses. And nobody shoot till I give the signal.'

Recruited by the Pinkerton Detective Agency the men in the grove were well-disciplined and capable of standing firm under fire. Guns were readied and ammo checked. Rifle sights were adjusted as the marksmen peered out at the nearing horde of outlaws.

'Remember, no shooting till my signal.'

Gwendolyn was tense as she stared out at the approaching pack. She checked her revolver and then the spare she had taken from the man she and Alice had jumped at the latrine. Carefully she tucked the spare back in her waistband. She was aware of Alice pressing close.

'Alice, perhaps you should drop back apiece. There's going to be bullets coming in here.'

If anything Alice snuggled closer. 'I can reload for you. You'll be too busy shooting.'

'Steady, men. Remember, surprise is our advantage. They outnumber us but each one of you is better than five of them.'

Jones and his men were in no hurry, confident they would soon be in sight of their quarry. It would be an easy kill; just a goddamn couple of kids against forty guns. After they disposed of them they would quench their thirst at the waterhole and ride back to Drygulch Canyon. Nobody double-crossed Ernest Jones and lived to boast about it. At a signal from Jones the horsemen slowed down to a walking pace. The grove of trees screening the waterhole was coming into focus.

'I'm hoping they make a stand at the waterhole,' Jones shouted across to Beniah Arnold. 'We can encircle them and pump lead in from all directions.'

Arnold pulled out his Colt and spun the cylinder. 'I'd rather get them alive and take them back to Drygulch. Make them squeal some afore we finish them off.'

'Depends on how much ammunition they have. We can sit out here while they fire at us. But we don't want any more casualties. One man dead and three injured. They might be kids but they still got a sting or two left in them. We got time on our side. If necessary we pen them here and come night we sneak in.'

The grove of trees at the watering hole looked silent and deserted as the horsemen approached. The outlaws had drawn guns and were scanning the trees alert for a sight of their quarry. Nothing stirred; not even a bird was evident.

Jones turned and signalled his men. 'We'll hole up here and water the horses. I want a couple of men riding ahead keeping those goddamn varmints in sight.'

As Ernest Jones shouted his instructions, Nathanial Shaler called out to the deputies hidden in the trees.

'Now!' he yelled. 'Kill those goddamned sons of bitches!'

As the last syllables left Shaler's lips every man in the Pinkerton force let loose with his weapon. It was a fearsome and devastating fusillade. The outlaws were caught completely by surprise. Expecting a couple of green kids to oppose them, instead they encountered a small army of lawmen.

Gwendolyn fired into the confused mass of horsemen. She could see Ernest Jones to the forefront and aimed her shots at him. This was the man who had killed her father and destroyed her life. She squeezed the trigger of her weapon till the hammer fell on empty. Immediately she threw down the revolver, hardly noticing as Alice snatched it up again and reloaded.

The noise within the grove was shockingly loud as guns kept up a continuous barrage. There was no mercy shown. Every lawman there knew the character of the brutes they were dealing with. Jones and his mob were cruel butchers who had murdered and raped their way across several states. Just as Jones had shown no mercy to his victims so too the lawmen were ruthless in dealing with the killers now exposed to their guns.

Dead and wounded outlaws were tumbling from their mounts, sprawling in the dirt and being trampled by panicked horses. Miraculously, Jones was still atop his horse, firing back at the ambushers and shouting at his men to retreat. Beniah Arnold was shot several times before he succumbed to the weight of lead hitting him and pitched from his horse, dead before he hit the ground.

Half the outlaw force was wiped out in the first few minutes of the battle. Many turned to ride away only to be hit as they turned their backs on the attackers. A handful of riders did manage to ride away but few escaped unscathed.

Eager to finish off the survivors, the Pinkerton men left the cover of the trees and moved towards the jumble of horses and men, firing point blank into the hapless mass of animals and humans. The outlaws stood no chance. They had been relaxed and off-guard when the first fusillade hit them, cutting down several of their members before they knew what was happening. They tried to turn their mounts around only to be hampered by unhorsed men and riderless horses.

Shaler's men showed no let up. Their killing lust was roused and they were unstoppable as they fired volley after volley into the milling horsemen. As many horses died as did their riders.

Gwendolyn stopped firing when her second gun was empty. Alice pressed the reloaded spare into her hand but Gwendolyn could not fire it. She stared in fascinated horror as the slaughter went on and then she could look no more but bent her head and stayed like that, trying to block out the harrowing sights as the outlaws were cut to ribbons under the withering firepower of the Pinkerton men. She heard someone calling out.

'Cease fire! Cease fire!'

The rate of firing slowed then petered out altogether.

The lawmen kept their weapons ready as they stared at the carnage they had created; dead and wounded men and animals strewn where they had fallen.

The silence as the firing ceased was almost as deafening as the barrage that had preceded it till the horrendous screaming of the wounded men and beasts burst upon their hearing.

36

The Pinkerton men survived the battle of Little Buffalo waterhole relatively unscathed. One deputy was dead and two of their number sustained minor flesh wounds. Of the gang of outlaws who had pursued the escapees, twenty-four were dead and five wounded men were taken prisoner.

'No sigh of Jones among the dead, then.'

'Nope, that varmint has the luck of the Devil. Still, we've thinned out his gang a mite.'

'So many deaths,' Sheriff Quigley observed sombrely, staring out over the carnage. 'I suppose in a way it is apt revenge for my brother Harold.'

'Revenge is a kind of wild justice, which the more man's nature runs to the more ought law to weed it out,' Shaler quoted.

Sheriff Quigley glanced quizzically at the detective. 'A kind of wild justice; is that Shakespeare?'

'Francis Bacon. I've been thinking, if we push on now we can storm Drygulch Canyon and once and for all put an end to that scourge. With so many of his men dead, Jones will have a hard time defending that hellhole. What do you think?'

'Count me in.'

'Mount up, men,' Shaler called. 'We're going to smoke out the rest of those vermin.' He spied Gwendolyn standing by while the wagon was being loaded and headed over. 'Glen Caruthers,' Shaler stuck out his hand, 'you are one hell of a law officer. It was solely by your efforts we finally broke Ernest Jones and his gang. As soon as I get back, I'll be asking my agency to award you a medal for bravery and I'm sure the government will want to acknowledge you also.'

'Can't you extend the award to include him?' Gwendolyn pointed to Ben, seated in the wagon. 'I couldn't have done it without the help of Ben Truman.'

Shaler called over Sheriff Quigley. 'Glen here reckons he couldn't have busted out of the canyon without the help of Truman.'

'So he tells me. And to his credit Truman did save Mrs Blatch and her daughter.'

'He saved me as well,' interposed Gwendolyn. She was thinking furiously. How could she make Ben out to be more than a mere outlaw who just happened along for the ride? In the short time she had known him she had grown overly fond of him. Maybe there was a way to save him from his life of crime. 'When Truman found out I was a lawman he kept his mouth shut. Jones near beat him to death to make him tell but he refused to inform on me.' As she told the lies, Gwendolyn couldn't look in Ben's direction for fear of betraying herself. 'And Ben tells me he was railroaded into prison on false testimony. I'm inclined to believe him. We sure owe him.'

'That's settled then. I'm making him your responsibility. When I get back I'll see about reviewing his previous conviction.'

The wounded outlaws were loaded on the wagon and

Gwendolyn, with Alice sitting alongside her, started the drive back to Fullerton escorted by two of Sheriff Quigley's deputies.

'I reckon I fall more and more into your debt, Glen Caruthers,' Ben spoke to Gwendolyn's back as she drove the cart. 'First you save my life and now you made me into some kind of hero. But that don't change nothing. I still owe you a hiding.'

Alice, sitting beside Gwendolyn whirled around. 'You ungrateful brute, you dare put a finger on Glen an' you'll have me to deal with.'

This outburst gave Alice an excuse to put a protective arm around Gwendolyn and snuggle close. Gwendolyn shifted uncomfortably under her embrace.

'Shucks,' complained Ben, 'I ain't no match for both of you. I guess I'll just have to get Glen on his lonesome some dark night.'

And in spite of herself Gwendolyn could not help but feel a tiny frisson of pleasure at the thought of Ben and her alone somewhere on a dark night, but she quickly suppressed the thought.

Though it was late when they reached Fullerton the townsfolk came out in force to greet them. The wounded were taken to the sawbones to be patched up while the survivors made their way to the saloon to celebrate the famous victory over the Jones gang. Quigley's deputies were the centre of attention as they relived lurid details of the gun battle for the entranced listeners.

Gwendolyn could not shake Alice, who clung to her rescuer like a shadow. She was only relieved of the strain of keeping the avid young woman at bay when her mother arrived on the scene. It was a tearful reunion and Mrs Salinger alternately hugged Gwendolyn and her daughter till she was breathless.

'You sure are a real ladies' man,' Ben remarked as he watched Mrs Salinger drag her daughter home to fuss over her now she had her back again. 'I sure hope I get an invite to the wedding.'

'What are you talking about!' snapped Gwendolyn. 'I'm off for some shut-eye.'

She stomped off to the hotel in the hope of finding a bed for the night. The hotel was full.

'Damn,' she swore uncharacteristically. 'Looks like a livery stable again.'

Gwendolyn never quite reached the stables. A bulky figure stepped out from the boardwalk.

'Sheriff Tomalley!' Events had moved so fast Gwendolyn had forgotten all about the fat lawman and his connection to Jones. 'I'm just looking for a place to bed down.' Then she saw the gun in the sheriff's hand. 'What's going on. . . ?'

'I got someone as wants to talk to you. Don't make a fuss otherwise I'll shoot you down and claim you jumped me. Hand that gun over.'

With the spare gun tucked into his expansive waistband Tomalley directed Gwendolyn to walk ahead of him till eventually they arrived at the livery.

'Here he is, just as you asked,' Tomalley called to someone inside, invisible amongst the shadows.

A match flared and a lamp was lit. Gwendolyn stared in horror at the man who had fired the lamp. Ernest Jones leered at her.

'You son of a bitch, you sure fooled me coming in with Perkins. It was a clever ploy. But I don't ever allow no one to cross me. You and I have a reckoning to settle.' Jones came close and stared into her eyes. Gwendolyn quailed before that baleful look. 'I could kill you now but that would be too easy. I need time to make you regret you ever crossed my path.

'We only need to nab Truman to complete the duet. I

want to hear you songbirds sing for me. You are both going to die but I want to make it as painful as possible for you. Take him out the back. The horses are saddled and ready.'

Sheriff Tomalley shoved Gwendolyn. 'It'll be a pleasure, Ernest,' he said. 'I'm sure looking forward to hearing him squeal.'

When Gwendolyn departed Ben was left alone. The celebrating citizens of Fullerton ignored him and Ben was suddenly aware of his isolation.

'Hell, I don't fit in nowhere.'

Suddenly his mind was made up. He would steal a horse and light out. His one regret was he would not be able to say goodbye to Glen. He felt a strong bond with the young lawman and it was with genuine sorrow he realized they would probably never meet again.

Leaving the Golden Nugget, Ben walked towards the livery where they had parked the wagon. Ahead of him he saw two figures and tried to identify them. One was slim and boyish and the other was big and bulky. Ben frowned as he realized the big man was holding a gun. Then he sucked in his breath as he recognized the man he was escorting.

'Glen, by God.'

Quickly Ben pulled his gun and followed.

37

As the pair he was following disappeared into the livery, Ben raced forward. He stood to one side of the doors and risked a peek inside but ducked back again as he heard his name spoken. A cold hand squeezed his insides as he recognized the voice of the speaker. Somehow Ernest Jones had survived and was in Fullerton, intent on revenge against the people he figured were the cause of his downfall. Ben pushed his gun inside the livery door. Without hesitation he fired at the man he was sure was Jones.

There was a curse and immediately the lamp was doused, plunging the interior of the livery into darkness. Jones swiftly returned fire. Bullets hammered into the frame of the door keeping Ben cowering outside.

He tried poking his gun inside without revealing himself and fired a couple of shots onto the livery. Again bullets smacked into the doorframe, sending splinters flying into the darkness. It was stalemate. As soon as Ben showed, he would be shot down.

Sheriff Tomalley spun round as the shots blasted out, leaving Gwendolyn momentarily unguarded. Propped against a stall was a pitchfork and she immediately grabbed this and swung round with it. Tomalley, sensing the movement, turned back to his captive.

'Drop that!' he yelled as he brandished his gun.

The pitchfork clenched in both hands, Gwendolyn was already lunging towards the fat lawman. It was a charge born of desperation and in her eagerness she tripped and fell just as Tomalley fired. Something hit Gwendolyn a tremendous blow in the chest and the pitchfork was wrenched from her hands.

She fell, feeling incredible pain biting at her and constricting her breathing. Gasping she tried to get up but weakness and the dreadful hurting kept her on the ground. The darkness of the night crept across her eyes and the pain ebbed along with consciousness.

Sheriff Tomalley blundered back squealing like a wounded

animal, the tines of the pitchfork embedded in his belly.

'Help me!' he bawled. 'Oh, God, someone help!'

Crouched outside the livery Ben heard the racket and taking a chance, looked inside. There was a flash of a gunshot. Something hit the doorway and splinters of wood stung his cheek. Ben instinctively ducked back but kept his gun aimed inside and fired till he clicked on empty. Hastily he began to reload wondering at the same time if he should retreat. But then the thought of leaving Glen at the mercy of Jones kept him at his post.

The howling of someone in mortal pain continued and a bulky figure staggered into the doorway. Ben looked up as he saw the man clutching bloody hands across his huge expansive of stomach.

'Oh God help me! Someone help. . . .'

The man dropped to his knees and began sobbing. With a freshly loaded gun Ben leapt across to the moaning man. Bullets stitched the night around him but he made it to the shelter of the bulky figure kneeling in the doorway of the livery. Inside he saw the flashes as Jones fired.

Ben took careful aim over the shoulder of his human shield. He had a clear shot and he could not miss. Once, twice, three times he fired and saw Jones staggering back. Even as the bandit was hit he was still triggering shots at his opponent. Sheriff Tomalley jerked as bullets hammered into his broad back then fell forward, knocking Ben to the ground. There was silence, broken by the sound of boots running towards the livery as townsfolk came to see what the shooting was all about.

Ben Truman sat in the doctor's outer room twisting his hat in his hand and staring morosely at nothing.

'Goddamn you, Glen Caruthers, don't you die on me,' he muttered.

And try as he might he could not help the moistening of his eyes. With an irritated gesture he wiped his sleeve across his face, then went back once more to twisting his hat into shapelessness.

The door opened and Doctor Black, a stately greybeard, stepped inside. Ben jumped to his feet and stared anxiously at the sombre figure of the medical man.

'You'll be pleased to know, we got the bullet out. The young woman is weak at the moment but she's young and healthy and I've no doubt she'll make a full recovery.'

'But what about Glen?' Ben asked. 'The fella as we brought in with the gunshot wound.'

'You seem a mite confused. Perhaps I should examine you.'

'No, no, you don't understand. It's Glen I'm worried about; with the bullet in his chest.'

'Young man, there is only one patient in this place. The young woman with the bullet wound, as you describe. The others at the scene were dead and beyond my help.'

'Woman?' Ben was staring in consternation at the doctor. He staggered back and leant against the wall. 'Wha . . . what are you saying?'

'Let me make myself clear. You brought in a young female with a bullet wound. I have extracted the bullet and her condition is comfortable. Are you a relation?'

Ben's mouth gaped open as he took in the doctor's words.

'You mean Glen is female? You sure you ain't made a mistake?'

Doctor Black drew himself up straight. 'Young man, I've been a medical man all my life. I can assure you I am sufficiently qualified to tell the difference between the male and female physique.'

'Goddamn my grandmother's parents. Can I see him . . . her?'

'Very briefly. She's still very weak.'

Doctor Black led the way into a bedroom. 'I'll be back shortly. Try not to tire her.'

Suddenly shy, Ben stood by the bed and stared down at the pale face of the patient.

'Glen.'

He got a wan smile in return and suddenly Ben felt a warm glow of affection flooding his body.

'I . . . you . . . you ain't Glen, are you?'

'Please, I don't want to talk about it.'

Suddenly Ben was on his knees beside the bed. 'Ever since I met you I felt there was some kind of bond between us. Until now, I never knew why. I just believed it was the tie of comradeship. Now I know you're a woman I feel an attachment to you as I never thought I would with anyone. I don't know why you pretended to be Glen Caruthers . . . but . . . but . . . I want you to know I will never forget you and all you did for me. Just tell me your real name and I can go away content with that name in my heart. Maybe some day when I clear my name I can come back and . . . and. . . .'

Ben trailed off, embarrassment warring with all the other emotions within him. Gwendolyn had turned her face away from him and he felt the force of her rejection.

'I . . . I'm sorry for intruding.' He stood up to go. 'Goodbye . . . Glen. . . .'

He was at the door before she said her name. 'Gwendolyn.'

It stopped him. 'Gwendolyn,' he murmured as he grasped the door knob. 'Thank you, Gwendolyn. I will treasure that name always.'

'You can't come back, Ben.'

'I know. I . . . I guess you wouldn't want to have nothing to do with an escaped convict and outlaw.'

'No . . . no . . . you don't understand! It's not you – it's me. I ain't fit for to be with no man.'

Ben turned back to look at her. 'Hell, just because you dressed as a fella it ain't no reason to be ashamed. It don't make no difference to me.'

'They took me—'

'Took you, who took you – where?'

'I'm a spoiled woman. Ernest Jones came by our farm. Killed pa . . . and . . . and. . . .'

There was a sob in her voice. The door opened.

'Time's up, young fella. I'll have to ask you to leave and let the lady get some rest.'

'Wait . . . wait. . . .' Ben was again kneeling by the bed. Gwendolyn's face was turned to the wall. 'A woman perjured me into prison and I swore I could never believe in any female ever again. Then you come along and not only save my life but, I . . . you . . . you're a . . . hell damnit, I love you.' The words were blurted out and Ben knelt by the bed, his face flushed and his heart pounding with inner turmoil.

Gwendolyn turned to him. He saw the tears in her eyes and tentatively reached out and touched the moistened cheek.

'I'll be here when you're ready,' he whispered.

Behind Ben the doctor cleared his throat. Slowly Gwendolyn reached up and took his hand. For long moments they stared into each other's eyes.

'Yes,' she said simply.